Praise for
CHURCH OF THE DOG

"*Church of the Dog* is a radiant novel that honors the broken among us, tenderly healing with its love, humor, and understanding. It's a classic on the spirituality of everyday life."
—Luanne Rice, *New York Times*
bestselling author of *Light of the Moon*

"What a rollicking, inviting, eccentric novel this is!"
—SARK, Author & Artist, SUCCULENT WILD WOMEN

"This is a sweet, whimsical tale of love and friendship, a slice of pure life. It is a beautiful story that is not to be missed."
—Lynne Hinton, author of
Friendship Cake and *The Arms of God*

"What a genuinely surprising novel Kaya McLaren has written, with characters that are each, in their own way, quietly magical and also heartbreakingly true. Like Barbara Kingsolver's early heroines, Mara O'Shaunnessey lives in the real world but reminds us, in all her actions, that animals can be messengers of truth and love has transformative powers."
—Cammie McGovern, author of *Eye Contact*

"The magic and wit and attention to place in Kaya McLaren's impressive first novel come together in a dance all their own. And don't let the smallness of the book fool you, it's big-hearted in the best sense of the word."
—Myra McLarey, author of *Water from the Well*

"With prose as clear and pure as mountain water, Kaya McLaren has written a testament to the plain sense of things. *Church of the Dog* is spiritual, even a little magical, but it's also incredibly practical. A lovely, uplifting book."
—Sarah Addison Allen, author of
Garden Spells and *The Sugar Queen*

"Kaya McLaren's sincere and generous feelings for all the creatures of this world make this novel of comforting magic both heartfelt and heartening."
—Christina Schwarz, author of *Drowning Ruth* and *All Is Vanity*

PENGUIN BOOKS

CHURCH OF THE DOG

Kaya McLaren lives and teaches on the east slope of Snoqualmie Pass in Washington State. When she's not working, she likes to telemark ski, sit in hot springs, moonlight hike, and play in lakes with her dog, Big Cedar.

church of the dog

KAYA McLAREN

PENGUIN BOOKS

PENGUIN BOOKS

Published by the Penguin Group

Penguin Group (USA) Inc., 375 Hudson Street, New York, New York 10014, U.S.A.
Penguin Group (Canada), 90 Eglinton Avenue East, Suite 700, Toronto,
Ontario, Canada M4P 2Y3 (a division of Pearson Penguin Canada Inc.)
Penguin Books Ltd, 80 Strand, London WC2R 0RL, England
Penguin Ireland, 25 St Stephen's Green, Dublin 2,
Ireland (a division of Penguin Books Ltd)
Penguin Group (Australia), 250 Camberwell Road, Camberwell,
Victoria 3124, Australia (a division of Pearson Australia Group Pty Ltd)
Penguin Books India Pvt Ltd, 11 Community Centre,
Panchsheel Park, New Delhi – 110 017, India
Penguin Group (NZ), 67 Apollo Drive, Rosedale, North Shore 0632,
New Zealand (a division of Pearson New Zealand Ltd)
Penguin Books (South Africa) (Pty) Ltd, 24 Sturdee Avenue,
Rosebank, Johannesburg 2196, South Africa

Penguin Books Ltd, Registered Offices:
80 Strand, London WC2R 0RL, England

First published in the United States of America by Daybue Publishing 2000
This revised edition published in Penguin Books 2008

1 3 5 7 9 10 8 6 4 2

Copyright © Kaya McLaren, 2000, 2008
All rights reserved

Publisher's Note
This is a work of fiction. Names, characters, places, and incidents either are the product
of the author's imagination or are used fictitiously, and any resemblance to actual persons,
living or dead, business establishments, events, or locales is entirely coincidental.

LIBRARY OF CONGRESS CATALOGING IN PUBLICATION DATA
McLaren, Kaya.
Church of the dog / Kaya McLaren.—rev. ed.
p. cm.
ISBN 978-0-14-311342-3
1. Friendship—Fiction. 2. Oregon—Fiction. I. Title.
PS3613.C57C48 2008
813'.6—dc22   2008008891

Printed in the United States of America
Set in Adobe Garamond • Designed by Elke Sigal

To Gram (Evelyn Green), my faith-keeper

ACKNOWLEDGMENTS 2000

Thank you to everyone who encouraged me to write, especially my uncles, Scott, Rick, and Doug, Aunt Trish, Elizabeth and Brian Frederick, and Karen and Doug Harris.

Thanks to my parents who raised me to believe I could do anything.

I'd especially like to thank all my students who were in reality my teachers and whom I love more than they will ever know.

Thanks to Gram, Char, Tess, Sue, and Jamie for reading my first draft before I sent it off. Thanks to Raymond Teague from Unity Books for his encouragement and enthusiasm. I'd like to thank my original editors, Elizabeth and Chris Day, who helped me become a better writer.

Last, I'd like to thank Tasha Good Dog for inspiring me and for watching over me like an Angel.

ACKNOWLEDGMENTS 2007

When you know better, you do better, and so this book went through another phase of growth since its original publication.

Thanks to all the book groups who read it and invited me to meetings. I thought about the things you said and the questions you had, and you are the biggest reason for this new incarnation.

Thanks to Meg Ruley and Christina Hogrebe at the Jane Rotrosen Agency for changing my life. Every day I thank my lucky stars for you. Thank you, Kendra Harpster, for being my partner in creativity and for using your powerful pit bull Mojo to make miracles happen for this book.

Thank you to the people who shared their experiences with

me: Savannah Davidson, my cousin who spent summers working on her dad's boat in Alaska; Mary Roberts, third-generation rancher; Andee Hansen and her husband, Sandy, who have driven to and from Alaska several times; and Jan Covey whose husband in Heaven gave her auto repair counsel.

I'd like to thank Bill Hawk, my high school English teacher, who taught me to write well, and Julie Sommers, my high school creative writing teacher, for her strong encouragement.

Tasha Good Dog went to Heaven in 2001, but I like to think she guided me to my next dog angel, Big Cedar, who sits by my side as I write this. Thanks to everyone who made it possible for the Sun Valley Animal Shelter to be a no-kill facility so that he was still alive when I finally answered the call. There are a lot of dog angels in shelters waiting for you to embrace them, people. Go out and adopt them.

CHURCH OF THE DOG

SUMMER

MARA

My car is packed with boxes and bags,
full of my hopes and dreams
and my disappointments
as I leave this man.
It wasn't supposed to be like this.
This wasn't how it was supposed to end.
But I say to myself, Hey, we all do the best we can.
And I say, So this is freedom.
I gave back the ring he gave to me,
and I gave back his hopes and dreams,
and I cry a little at their death.
I think of how he felt when he bought it.
I think of how he was when he gave it.
The love in his eyes and the shortness of his breath.
But, hey, this is freedom.
I take one last look at his big red dog in the driveway.
That dog was the only reason I said hi.
And I look at my garden, the things that I planted;
my hopes and my dreams.

I dig up my favorites, irises and lilies,
and leave the rest behind.
And I say, So this is freedom. So this is what it's like.
Hey, this is freedom.
I got what I wanted—I got back my life.
So I walk up to you and decide not to kiss you good-bye.
But I take one last look, and I wave as I drive out of sight.

❧

I am transplanting my hopes and dreams into my Gram's garden. They look like irises and lilies, but they feel like my soul, and I couldn't leave it all behind. He took enough of my soul. Right now it feels like it will never grow back, but I know that just like the irises will reproduce every year, spreading to fill in the empty spaces in the garden, so will my soul. Gram is not much of a gardener. I know my soul won't be hacked back, trimmed, or subjected to control in any form. Gram has always known what my soul needs. I call her my faith keeper.

She opens the back door, sees me, puts on her jacket, and smiles as she walks over. "I thought I heard a garden spirit at work out here!"

"I figured you wouldn't mind giving my flowers some sanctuary," I say.

"Not at all."

"I couldn't leave them behind."

"Oh." Although she doesn't ask, I can tell she's curious about why I canceled my engagement.

"The other night I had an allergic reaction and needed to be taken to the hospital in the middle of the night. He drove me, and the whole time I'm thinking what a good friend he is, because the hospital is an hour away, and he was so kind. At the end of the week, though, he was doing bills and tallying my half of everything. At the bottom of the weekly bill he created for me, there was a ten-dollar charge for gas used to take me to the hospital." I could go into how it was symbolic of how he kept score, of how he always feared not having enough or not getting what he felt was due him, but I won't open that can of worms. "I almost married a man who charged me ten bucks for a trip to the hospital. I wouldn't charge a stranger ten bucks for a trip to the hospital."

Gram erupts in laughter. "Did you pay it?"

"Yes, I paid it. Best ten bucks I ever spent. Now I can leave without going through the courtesy of trying to be friends. I don't owe him anything. I can go and never, ever look back."

Gram, coming from another generation where men treated women differently, laughs and laughs about my ten-dollar charge. She laughs so hard, she can't speak. She laughs as she walks to the other side of the house to dump a bucket of weeds, and she laughs the whole way back.

"Mara," she manages to get out, "two words: *great escape*."

What I didn't tell her about the trip to the hospital is that . . . well, I don't know how to explain this. I think I brought a man back from the dead . . . twice.

I can see energy, but not all the time and not all of it. And you know, I didn't ask for this ability, and sometimes it really freaks me out. Most of the time I don't look for it. I figure it's none of my business. Sometimes, though, it's just there.

Anyway, I heard this code blue alarm going on next door, and I figured I didn't want to absorb anyone else's energy, so I started picturing white light coming out of the tops of fir trees, down through my head, and filling me with so much light that the excess poured out of my hands. Since I discovered this technique, I stopped passing out every time I got around someone with a disease or injury.

On that day, though, it wasn't working for some reason. I don't know why. Then, out of nowhere, I thought of the saguaro cacti in Arizona and pictured red light coming out of them and into me, just like in the other visualization.

The minute I started thinking about red light, the code blue alarms stopped. I held that thought for a few minutes, but then my mind wandered, and instantly the code blue alarm went off again. I thought of the cacti with the red light, and the alarms once again stopped.

I looked down at my own body that had been covered in huge hives just five minutes ago, as it had been for the last twelve hours, and was startled to see my skin almost completely clear. That was the moment I realized that even though I don't know much, I knew more about healing than the doctors or nurses ever would. I took off the stupid ID bracelet that had been hurting me and the crunchy gown that reeked of bleach and had been making my skin burn even more. I put my soft cotton flannel pajamas back on and ran like hell out of there.

❧

I'm figuring out that other people have this ability, too, only no one talks about it because none of us wants to be called crazy—especially when we often don't know how to interpret what we see.

This is why I love art. Art is the medium those of us who see the unexplainable converse in. It's safe. And those who don't see the neon dots floating around people, the sparkles falling from the sky, and the auras, of course, can just write it off as imagination and creativity. In that respect, it's a coded conversation.

For instance, last week I saw this artist's work in a gallery who is clearly one of us. She paints the energy of the forest. Vibrant. My eyes watered as I stared at her work. I felt so full of appreciation for our beautiful, alive planet, and knowing she understood eased my loneliness.

Naturally, I'm enthralled with light in my own art, which is why stained glass is my passion. I can appreciate the translucence of watercolor, but stained glass that actually uses light . . . oh, it takes my breath away. I spend a lot of time thinking about the existing great works of stained glass.

Historically, stained glass was used to teach illiterate people about the Bible, and while some images are nothing short of heavenly, some I find rather disturbing. If you, like me, are of the mind that everything is either love or fear, and you see that some of those windows promote fear while Jesus promoted love, you can see why I believe more windows are needed that truly represent the universal truths of love. These truths were articulated by all the great prophets. They're not that complicated. This is why I've dedicated my life to creating windows that show what God truly is: love, light, life, and the power of creation. I also try to create windows that convey how we are all connected by virtue of God residing within us all.

Perhaps saying I dedicate my life to creating spiritual windows was a bit hasty, because I certainly spend a fair amount of my life working as a public school art teacher. I get to teach young people to look at light and life. I get to encourage them to appreciate themselves, and appreciation is a form of love. I get to teach them to be kind to other living things, which is a way of acknowledging the God that resides in all living things. And I certainly get to help them learn about their own power of creation. In that respect, I see it as working in support of God. Therein lies happiness.

I confess, though, that today I'm not happy I'm a public school teacher because I'm working in support of God. No, today I'm happy to be a public school teacher because I have one and a half weeks of summer vacation left, and I'm off on a road trip to see the Grand Canyon.

ÐANIEL

It's the only letter I received all summer, the only time the captain handed me anything other than credit card offers. And there's not much to it. I look at it sticking out of the pocket on the shirt that hangs on the wall near my bed. The shirt sways as the boat rocks. Feels like a good-sized summer storm tonight.

On the other side of the room, Jack snores loudly. I'm obligated to pretend it bugs me, but really I like it. I like the sound of him living. Steve used to share this room with me before he was promoted to first mate. He slept too quietly. There were nights I'd wake up terrified that he had died, which I knew wasn't logical. I'd lie there in a state of panic and self-loathing until finally my anxiety grew so great that I would make myself get up and watch him breathe. With Jack I get to stay in my bed. There's no question he's breathing.

Steve knocks at the door, opens it, and looks at me. "Your turn."

I put on the flannel shirt with the envelope in the pocket, slip on my fleece pants, and climb the stairs to the wheelhouse as the boat continues to rock.

Fifty-foot waves splatter the windows of the wheelhouse, common in the winter but impressive in the summer. I take the wheel, and Steve staggers through the interior door and down the stairs to bed. I hold the wheel and watch the droplets of water from the waves hit the window. I don't like it. Then it begins to rain, and the rain hits the windows. I don't like that, either. I don't like any precipitation of any kind hitting any window. I especially don't like windshield wipers. But I hate snow. I hate the sight of snow hitting glass. I hate it.

I watch the radar and check the electronic charts and GPS to make sure our tender boat, a crab fishing boat in winter, stays away from icebergs and off sandbars and rocks, and that we stay on course. Tomorrow we'll deliver seventy thousand pounds of king salmon to the land plant in Valdez. Night duty in the wheelhouse is usually painful. Quiet. It's usually so damn quiet. At least the heavy sheets of water that pelt the window make noise. It's a tough toss-up what I can't stand more—silence or precipitation on windshields.

And then there's the envelope in my pocket. So much is wrapped up in that little envelope. Failure, mostly. My failure. My cowardice. The disappointment I've been to the only two people on this earth who love me. At least Grandpa's words are not kind. They're not unkind, but they're not kind. They're neutral. They're straightforward. And usually I can handle that, but this one contained a straightforward request: Come home. Come home to the land of my losses and failures, to my inadequacies and irrational fears. Come home to the people to whom I owe more than I could ever repay, to the people I abandoned. Come home.

I open it and reread it. He says nothing about my failures, nothing about the humiliation and confusion I caused him. He says nothing about forgiveness, either, but even if he offered it, I would have to believe they were just words. You can't forgive someone for just disappearing.

There is one thing I do like about piloting the ship at night. It's the reason I chose this life. It's the sense of disappearing all over again, disappearing into a night so dark I cannot be seen, in a sea so vast I cannot be found. I hold the wheel in the storm and just disappear.

EARL

"Dammit," I say as I nick the side of my neck. I reach for some toilet paper to stop the bright red blood that gushes out of the tiny cut and press the tissue hard into the cut. Under the cut I feel a lump, a little lump about the size of a gumball.

Maybe it's just the mother of all ingrown hairs . . . or a pimple. I haven't had a pimple since I was nineteen, but, still, it could be. Except the skin wasn't red on top of the lump. Ingrown hairs and pimples are red.

Hey, it's just a lump. My old dog, Blue, used to be covered with them. They were just fatty cysts. That's probably what this is, a cyst.

I try to move it with my finger. It doesn't move. Don't cysts move? I think cysts move. Did Blue's lumps move? I can't remember.

It could be a bone spur growing off the side of one of my neck vertebrae.

But what if it's not? What if it's the Grim Reaper stalking me from the inside out? Dammit. I look at my reflection in the mirror and see an old man. When'd I get to be such an old son of a bitch? When I was a boy, I used to pass men like me outside the feed store, and I used to think they looked like they had lived a good long life. I figured they were ready to die when God called out their number. Now I look just like them, and I can tell you, I do not feel ready to have my number called.

Such a small bump. Funny how the smallest things bring down the biggest beasts. Bullets. Germs. Cancer cells. Yeah, it's the small stuff that gets you.

I turned seventy-nine last May. I suppose seventy-nine is technically a good long life, but I figured I'd be kicking away at ninety-three like Henry O'Toole down the road, out there fixing fences and moving irrigation pipes. I figured I was at least as strong as Henry O'Toole. Seventy-nine is not that old. I mean, yes, it's not that young, either, but it's not even eighty. I'd like to make it to eighty.

I'm probably getting excited about nothin'. Probably just a cyst.

Seventy-nine isn't old, but it is too damn old to put myself at the mercy of my crack physician. The hospital is like a roach motel to us old people. You go in, but you don't come out. Seventy-nine is too old to put myself through chemo. If my days are numbered, I sure ain't gonna waste them puking. No, I ain't gonna live out my days in no goddamned hospital.

Plus, you gotta figure I'm gonna die anyway. No use rackin' up bills and losing the ranch trying to fight it.

Listen to me. This is ridiculous. It's a cyst. I leave the tissue sticking to the clotting blood on my neck and walk out of the bathroom.

I ain't gonna tell Edith about these bumps. No use in her worrying about it, especially since they're just cysts. Plus, you know, she'd make me go to the damn doctor.

EDITH

Earl sits at the dinner table with me. He chews his food and looks down at his plate. He is a man of few words, I suppose. In a way it's like living by myself, only with more work in some areas and less work in other areas. I glance at the wedding band on my finger and wonder if it's true, if I am really married. Faithful, yes, but celibate. Love? Sure. We've got history. Partners, absolutely. But friends? I mean, do I think Earl likes me? Not really. It's not that I think he dislikes me. I think I'm just part of his landscape, and he simply accepts and expects my presence. A long time ago his eyes sparkled when he looked at me. Now, nothing, nothing but same old, same old. I get up and do the dishes.

We're both tired from a long day of putting up silage. It's fast work, since we can't let the cut grass dry. Whitey's been coming out to help. I drive the swather with the self-propelled chopper that blows it into a big semi. Whitey drives the semi to the pit where he dumps it. Finally, Earl packs it down tight with a tractor. The compaction seals it and keeps it fresh. The fermentation process softens even the toughest weeds. Kimchi for cattle. It's high-energy food in the winter.

Earl goes back out to check on the contractors who have been swathing and baling our hay. They're good this year. We used to bring in our own hay, too, but ranch help is almost impossible to get anymore. It doesn't pay as well as the jobs in town. Most people who do it aren't particularly educated. I don't have anything against uneducated people, but a lot of uneducated people are also not particularly motivated or hardworking, and this is very hard work. Really, though, by the time we put up hay, pay fuel costs, and keep our machinery maintained, there isn't a lot left over to pay a hired hand anyway.

This isn't the most profitable business. We're able to make it because we own our land free and clear. Still, no one is in it to get rich. You have to love working with cattle. You have to love this life. I don't need much. For me, taking a moment to sit on a hill and just be in nature is as good as it gets. What I have is enough for me.

I put on my boots and go to the barn to check on a sick yearling I found yesterday. He had pulled off by himself. Cattle are herd animals, so that's always a red flag. His nose is still dry, he's still pulled up in the flank, and still humped off in the back. I give him a thousand cc's of penicillin. I remember when

I found him last spring. He didn't get on his mother's tit fast enough. They have just an hour or so to get that first colostrum milk in them. After that their bodies won't absorb it, and their chance at any kind of natural immunity is blown.

In a nearby corral are my two special calves. I check Ray Charles and Special K. Ray was born blind last spring. It took me a few days to figure it out. And I think Special K might have Down's syndrome. For whatever reason, they grew on me. I spent more time with these two calves than I did with the other twelve hundred that were born around the same time. I can't just turn them loose. They'd never make it. I told Earl I don't know what we're going to do with them, because I can't eat them.

Then I return to the house. Earl has already gone to bed and fallen asleep. I'm glad about that. It's nice to just go to bed in peace and not have to use one more ounce of energy, energy I don't have, to make polite conversation with someone who is also too tired to be polite. It's not easy to work together all day and sleep next to each other all night. We work well together, though. Earl doesn't yell at me. I hear the stories that other ranchers' wives tell about how their husbands yell at them when they're working cattle together, and I think, Gosh, I don't know what I would do if Earl yelled at me like that. Ride away, probably.

I look at his face for a moment before I turn off the light and lie down. He's a good man—not particularly interesting anymore, but good.

MARA

Hey, it's my birthday, so I stop in Sedona and visit a psychic. I like to get a taste of what I have to look forward to in the upcoming year. This one didn't talk about my future, though. She talked about my past. She talked about my dad.

"I don't care how old a person is, when they die, they feel sixteen again." She says this like it's fantastic to feel sixteen again. I confess I hope I don't feel sixteen again because sixteen wasn't all that great. "But they look down and see all their loved ones grieving, so they come to their loved ones in dreams to let them know they're okay. Only, Mara, you didn't wait for your loved ones on the other side to visit you in dreams. You were crossing over at a very young age to visit them . . . a grandmother and two grandfathers. And then later, after your father died, you were a regular."

It's true. I think back to all my dreams where I realized I was somewhere but didn't know where. But it was okay because the people were so friendly and the food was so delicious, it was indescribable. Oftentimes I looked for my father, and oftentimes I found him.

I leave Sedona and drive a little north. I'm pretty sure that all the campsites at the Grand Canyon are full, so I pull off on a dirt road. I open the back windows in case I need to escape into the locked safety of the cab in the night. I get out with my gear, unroll my sleeping pad onto the bed of my pickup, and throw my sleeping bag on it. I say my prayer: "God, Cosmos, Angels, and Guides, please clear me of all nonpositives. Please clear my friends and family of all nonpositives. Please keep a two-mile radius around me clear at all times. Please fill me and complete me with your light and love. Thank you for your guidance and protection. Please give my love to my family in Heaven. Thank you. Thank you for everything."

I love to sleep under the stars and listen to breezes in trees as I drift in and out of sleep.

At the crack of dawn I start driving north again until at last

I reach it. I arrive around five-thirty—before the rangers begin their day, so I enter for free, saving twenty much-needed dollars. I find a parking place near the edge, grab my guitar, and go in search of the perfect spot.

What no one can tell you about your first trip to the Grand Canyon is the inevitable revelation you are bound to have about time. All those lines going down the cliffs for what seems like infinity. We are such a tiny speck on the Grand Canyon time line.

I realize that in Grand Canyon years I am the same age as every single person on the planet today, and this realization gives me an overwhelming sense of unity.

As the sun begins to rise, I can see silhouettes of a few people up and down the canyon rim. Everyone is silent, seemingly in a state of reverence for this wonder of nature. I wonder if they, too, are feeling the unity or if they are still pondering their smallness.

I find the perfect spot and take out my guitar. I very quietly pluck some chord progressions, throwing in some harmonics here and there.

When the sun has risen, I decide to leave so that I remember the perfection of the last hour rather than the zoo it will become in another.

As I turn around to put my guitar in its case, I catch the eyes of a guy who apparently has been sitting not far from me, listening.

"Thanks," he says. His eyes are so bright that when I look at them, I feel the way I do after a movie matinee when I emerge from the dark theater into a bright day. I think, judging from those eyes, he sees what I do.

"You're welcome."

"Leaving?" He sounds disappointed.

"This has been such an incredible experience, I don't want it to be wrecked when thousands of international visitors in cowboy hats take over."

"Good point. Can I walk with you?" He has a sweetness about him and a clear, vibrant radiance. So although I usually don't let unfamiliar men anywhere near me, I say, "All right."

"I'm Adam," he says.

"Mara," I reply, and we shake hands.

"First time here?"

"Yeah. Yours?"

"No. I've come here every year on this day for the last two years to watch the sun rise."

"Hm. Birthday?" I ask.

"Actually, my brother died on this day three years ago."

"Sorry," I say, and he nods and looks at the ground. "Why here?"

"It's kind of hard to explain. To me the canyon is like a giant wound formed from the natural cycles of life, and what I find comforting about being here is people's acceptance of it. No one sits here and tells the Earth that time will heal this wound, and no one calls the processes that created it 'tragic.' No one expects the Earth here to be like it was before the river cut the canyon. People just leave it alone and find the beauty in it as it is."

I look him in the eye to let him know I understand. We sit, staring out at the canyon and reflecting in silence for a few minutes.

"Do you live nearby?" I ask.

"Triumph, Idaho. You?"

"I don't live anywhere right now. I just spent two years teaching on a reservation on the west side of the Olympic Peninsula in Washington State. In a couple weeks I'll be in a tiny town in northeastern Oregon. Right now I'm just trying to bleach out all the fungus that undoubtedly grew on me during the last two years."

He gives me one of those single laughs that is more like a smiling exhale. I love his vibrant glow.

"How long are you staying?" I ask.

"About another half hour," Adam replies. "What about you? Where are you headed next?"

"I don't know. I'd like to see Mesa Verde and Chaco Canyon, but I'd also like to avoid crowds."

"Try Hovenweep. It's small, but I think you'll like it. On both sides of the gulch are several small ruins that have peepholes so the residents could see their neighbors. Very few people go there because you have to drive on washboard dirt roads for a long time."

We reach my truck. "Thanks for the tip," I say. I'm distracted by the violet I see swirling around his head.

"Thanks for making my morning more beautiful," he says with sincerity, leaving me feeling flustered and awkward.

Somehow, leaving him doesn't feel natural, but I don't know what else to do. I mean, he is a stranger.

I step into my truck, but before I can say good-bye, he says, "I hope our paths will cross again."

"You just never know," I reply with a smile that surely reflects my conflicted feelings about leaving him, and shut the door.

As I back out of my parking space, he gives a little wave, and I give one back.

❧

A sign welcomes me to Three Hills, population 2,147. Actually, everyone who passed me on the road for the last twenty miles welcomed me. Every single person waved at me as they passed.

Every single one. The waves aren't big. They're usually just a finger or two lifted off the top of the steering wheel, but, still, it's congenial.

I feel like I've discovered a hidden valley and a world that hasn't existed since the fifties. Children play in the outdoor city swimming pool. Old men sit outside the feed store. The electric company is a co-op. I pass a park that sits in front of the elementary school, a library/historical museum, and a grocery store. On the other side of the street is the senior citizens' center, a drugstore, a bank, a fabric store, and another bank. People look friendly. On the left side there's an auto shop, Kate's Pizza and Video, the Elks Club, and a Les Schwab tire store. There's a dentist's office and a chiropractor's office, a bowling alley, and, up on the hill, a small hospital. On my way out of town I pass a graveyard, a concrete dam, and a small lake.

I love it. I love my new town. Good-bye, moldy, mossy, spongy, rainy forest. Good-bye, months and months and months of such thick clouds and darkness that a person can't see any colors outside. I'm living in the glorious sunshine now.

I drive at least ten miles beyond town, where the golden grass gives way to forested mountains. There, I turn down a dirt road and find a spot that looks acceptable for camping.

❦

"Hi, Gram," I say as she and I sit on a big rock just off the coast in my dream. The waves crash against us, tickling us with mist.

"Isn't this lovely?" she asks me, obviously enjoying the spot she chose. "I thought you'd like it." I smile and nod while she exhales and says with a sigh, "Oh, how I love the sea." She scans the horizon beyond the edge of the water. "So how are things going?" she asks.

"Oh, they're okay," I tell her.

"Found a place to live yet?" she asks.

"No, Gram, not yet," I reply.

"You will soon. Don't worry. I talked to your dad earlier, and he says it'll be obvious." She pats me on the shoulder to emphasize her reassurance. "Hey, some handsome fellow came looking for you in my dream the other night. . . . Said he met you at the Grand Canyon. . . . Ring any bells?" She gives me a wink.

"Did you like him?" I ask, a little shy.

"I liked him," she assures me.

This is how it goes. Gram and I meet in our dreams. We call them our vacations. I always let her pick the place. We end up at the ocean a lot. Then we go back to our bodies and finish sleeping.

Even before I open my eyes, I smell the sun warming the pine needles, releasing their fragrance. I love that smell. I crawl out of the bed of my truck and look through my big Tupperware box full of clothes for something to wear to the fair. It's been years since I've been to a fair, and it's a great opportunity to learn a little about my new community. I braid my hair and pour some water out of my water bottle onto my washcloth so I can wash my face and armpits. Then I brush my teeth, put on some sunblock, and drive into town.

I walk by the draft horses, my favorite, the sheep and goats, and then find myself at a hog auction watching a girl grieve for her hog as it's being auctioned off. It's like a car wreck, where despite the horror you can't stop watching. The other hogs went for about $2.50 a pound, but hers, being a runt, sells for only $2.35 a pound. Her EAT BEEF sign on the hog doesn't deter its sale as it appears she had hoped it would.

What a horrible tradition: Get the kids to invest their heart and soul raising an animal regarded as livestock, and then make them take their baby, their pet, their friend to the fair and sell it to people who will kill and eat it. Am I the only one who sees this as barbaric?

The girl is bordering on hysterical. She is being asked to pose in a picture with her hog and the people who bought it. She is supposed to feel pride from this experience, but she doesn't. She feels grief. And no one validates her grief, because to do so would require questioning the ethics of their lifestyle. It's much easier to rely on tradition than to question it.

I want that hog. Then I'll start a livestock sanctuary for all the mourning 4-H kids. They can sneak out to my farm to visit them, and when they are free from the oppression sometimes referred to as "childhood," they can take back their pet and live happily ever after. In my perfect world this is how it will work.

As they pose for the picture, the hog nuzzles her leg. I find myself crying at the hog auction, which is not such a good thing, and I use my long hair to try to hide my face from the farmers sitting around me.

"Hey, girl, you okay?" the guy sitting next to me asks. I nod without looking at him and walk away.

I want to steal that hog. I want to ride around on horses with a group of vegetarian cowgirls, stealing little kids' farm pets (with the kids' help and consent) and taking them to the farm pet sanctuary before their parents can make them sell them for slaughter.

The girl is getting tired now. Her face is white, and her lack of energy makes her seem very small all of a sudden. She begins to seem a little invisible to me as the future pet eaters walk away with her baby. The hog looks back at her, and I know she will never forget this moment.

I know this experience is supposed to teach her something good about money, and I'm sure for many less sensitive kids it does. But what they just taught her is that money is something you get when you betray your friends and betray your heart, and, therefore, good people don't have money. I'm willing to bet she'll resist prosperity for a long, long time. I mean, if money hurts this much, why would she want it?

I run up to the hog eaters. "I'll give you $2.45 a pound for that hog," I announce.

The obese man with the seed company hat looks at me like I'm nuts.

"Please," I say.

He looks at my undoubtedly bloodshot eyes and says, "Sold."

I walk the hog over to where the girl's mother is holding her. "Excuse me," I start. She looks up. "I just wanted to let you know I'm a vegetarian, and I just bought your hog." She and her mom start to laugh. I'm not sure whether they're laughing because they're relieved or whether they're laughing at me because I'm a vegetarian who just bought a hog.

"His name is Harvey," the girl says. "I'm Emily."

"Barbara McDougal," her mother introduces herself.

"Mara. Mara O'Shaunnessey," I say and shake their hands. "I'm the new art teacher here in town."

"You'll be my teacher!" Emily says.

"When I get settled, you'll be welcome to visit Harvey. Hey, I've never had a hog before. Anything I should know?"

"He likes Oreos. And he likes it when you scratch his belly. Be careful when you open a gate, because he'll knock you over trying to get out. He gets lonely. And he likes dogs. And if you have to give him medicine, put it inside a Twinkie and he'll eat it right up."

"Got it," I say. "See you in a couple days, I guess!" I walk the hog toward the door, but before I make it out, I hear a slightly familiar voice.

"You just bought yourself a pet, didn't you?" It's the man who had been sitting next to me.

I just smiled.

"Dang, girl. What are you gonna do with a hog if you ain't gonna eat it?"

"Ride it around when my pickup breaks, I suppose," I answer.

"You probably live in a city, too, right? Oh, your neighbors are gonna love you."

"Oh, even better. I don't live anywhere." I laughed. My heart sure gets me into some real pickles.

"So where are you going to keep your new pet?" He was clearly enjoying giving me a bad time, or he was beyond fascinated by what he probably regarded as the most stupid and impulsive act he had ever witnessed.

"Your place for the time being, I guess," I replied jokingly.

To my surprise he paused and thought about it. "That might work. I'd need to run it by my dad first. Family ranch. Name's Tim Grennan." He held out his hand.

"Mara. I'm the new art teacher in town."

"Tell you what. Let's just go. It's easier to ask for forgiveness than permission, and I think if my dad sees how pretty you are, he'll forgive me for bringing a pet hog home."

I follow Tim to my hog's new home. Just as we turn off the road onto his driveway, I notice a glow coming from just up the road. I can just barely see the top of a house.

❦

I back up to the chute Tim points to. Then I get out, drop my tailgate, and untie Harvey. He runs down the chute and searches the nearest trough for anything that may have been left behind. I realize I'm going to have to feed him somehow.

"The guys at the feed store will set you up. You just tell them the whole story of how you got this hog, and when they stop laughing, they'll get you exactly what you need," Tim says.

"I'm on it," I say with a big smile. "Hey, who lives over there?" I point to the glow.

"Edith and Earl McRae. Nice folks." He spits. "Hey, they have an old employee bunkhouse but no employees. I don't know what kind of shape it's in. They might be willing to rent it to you."

That is all I need to hear.

EARL

I stop at the window at the end of the upstairs hall and look out over part of my ranch. Twenty-six thousand acres. Twelve hundred cow-calf pairs. My ranch. It's so strange to think that one day it won't be my ranch. I won't be making the calls. I won't be looking after it. Would Edith sell it? She couldn't run it alone. I always wanted Daniel to have it, but seein' as he moved a quarter of the world away, I doubt he would want to spend the rest of his life looking after it. Too bad. It's a good life, an honest life. Gets you out of bed every morning. No boss man barkin' at you.

I think about all the old houses I pass on my drives, old houses falling to the ground because a neighbor bought the ranch for the land and had no use for the house. One day there's a leak in the roof, and the next it's a pile of rubble. What if that happens? What if this house where I've lived my whole life just falls to the ground? What if the next person undoes everything I spent my life doing?

Twenty-six thousand acres. Do you know how much land

that is? Do you got any idea how much land that is? Better yet, do you got any idea how much fencing that is? Won't be long before the ground is frozen. I'd better get on it just as soon as we're done with the silage.

What if I'm really sick? What if one day I'm out there fixing fences and then, boom, gone. I don't wanna die alone somewhere on my land with my wife, Edith, worryin' and turkey vultures pickin' at me so that when she finds me, I'm an awful disturbing mess. I don't wanna spend money she'll need when I'm gone to hire out to fix fences, but I also don't wanna leave her with bad fences.

I need some help around here. I need Daniel. I gotta get Daniel back home.

Then I notice a goddamned foreign pickup in my driveway. What the hell? Now who in their right mind would buy a goddamned foreign pickup? What the hell do the Japanese know about what a ranch demands of a truck? Are there even any cattle in Japan? I honestly do not know.

Out from the truck steps a very tall redhead, about six feet tall, wearing cowboy boots. I walk down the stairs and go out onto the porch with Edith.

"Hi. I'm Mara O'Shaunnessey. I'm the new art teacher."

"You're the vegetarian with a new pet hog," I say, trying to repress my laughter. "You're famous in these parts."

"Four hours. That spread fast." She nods and smiles at herself like a good sport.

Edith is smiling politely. There's a pause. "I'm Edith McRae, and this is my husband, Earl."

I wanna just ask her what she wants, but in an attempt not to humiliate my wife, I keep my mouth shut. I also wanna ask her what the hell my tax dollars are going to art for, but I keep my mouth shut on that one, too.

"Welcome, dear. Would you like some iced tea?" God love Edith.

"Um, . . . sure," says the redhead, suddenly all awkward.

Edith goes to get a glass. The redhead looks more and more awkward. She studies Edith's garden.

"What'd you say your name was?" I can't remember those damned hippie names.

"Mara."

Edith appears with the tea.

"Thank you," Mara says.

"So, Mara, what brings you to our ranch?" Edith asks. If I had asked that, it would have sounded unwelcoming.

Everything that comes from Edith's lips is so gentle and kind. Sometimes, I wish, that in my sixty years with her I coulda become a little more like her instead of just allowin' her to be that part of me for me. She's kind. I'm cranky. Together we make a whole person.

"Well, Tim next door watched my impulsive purchase of my new pet and for some reason took pity on me and offered to let me keep it over there," she begins.

"For some reason? Be careful or you'll end up being that boy's next wife," Edith warned, although it came off sounding like a joke.

"Yeah," she said uncomfortably, like she understood. "Well, I told him I was looking for a place to rent. . . ."

"Where are you staying now?" asks Edith.

"Camping east of here," Mara replies. "Weather's nice. I don't mind it at all. I'd like to be in a building by winter, though. And Tim mentioned that your ranch has some old employee quarters that are vacant. . . . Would you be interested in renting them to me?"

"Ever rode a horse?" I pipe up.

"Yes, sir."

"Know anything about fixin' fences?"

"No, sir."

"Know anything about fixin' anything?"

"Yes, sir."

"You afraid of hard work?"

"No, sir."

"I need help fixing fences and working cattle more than I need money. Interested?"

"I have more time than money, so, yes, very interested."

"Follow me. I'll show you your new home. Your hog can live in that pen. Can't have you marrying the Grennan boy. He's no good."

Problem solved. And when I'm gone, Edith will have a neighbor.

ᛏANIEL

While I scrub the tanks, the other crew members scrub other parts of the boat. It's our last day for a month. In October we'll come back for a three-week king crab season. After that, we'll be free again until January—snow crab season. Finally, in late February or early March, we'll be free once more until the end of May, the beginning of salmon again. Salmon is by far the longest season, and we're all eager to get off the boat. We like each other and work well together, but we're looking forward to not seeing each other for a while.

After I clean each of the four larger tanks and the two smaller ones, I'm done. I go back to my quarters, put my camera bag over my head and one shoulder, pick up my duffel bag, and walk off the boat.

I stop by the company office and find the mailbox with our

boat's name on it. I sort through it all, looking for anything for me. Aside from a couple of credit card offers, I find no evidence that the outside world has missed me at all, and then I get to an envelope from Three Hills, Oregon. Grandma. I stick it in my pocket, rip up the rest of my junk mail, and go back outside to sit on a bench and read what she has written.

It's a birthday card with a fish on it. "Today's a day that's just for you, to do the things you love to do! Happy Birthday!" Underneath the printed message, Grandma wrote, "Happy 29th, Daniel. We love you! Grandma and Grandpa."

My birthday was nine days ago. I didn't tell the guys. I didn't want anyone to contemplate whether they were glad I was born. I look at Grandma's writing. She's glad. I don't know whether anyone else is, but she is.

I take out my wallet and pull out two pictures. The top one is of me between my grandparents after I qualified for regional finals in bull riding. In the picture, taken just after I rode a huge Brahman named Tornado Joe, Grandpa looks proud while Grandma looks scared. I never noticed her fear before. The other picture, the one I keep tucked under the first, is of me sitting in my father's lap and driving the green Ford pickup around the circular driveway near my grandparents' barn. Mom and Dad are laughing.

Later, in the same truck with the same people, I would be crushed by silence. The silence would be more crushing than the countless rolls that left us upside down.

Like I did then, I shut my eyes tightly to try to block out what I wish I had never seen. I put the pictures back in my wallet and get up.

I cross the street that runs along the water and walk up another street to where a wooden sidewalk traverses a hill. Near the top I see my house, the ugliest house on the street, and hear my housemates' music. As I approach the door, I see Minda and Rob through the window, dancing wildly. I can smell the stink of our house even before I open the door.

"Hey, Daniel! It's Devo Night!" Minda shouts and hugs me as I walk through the door. Although Minda is like a sister to me, she's also the first woman I've seen in a month. She's a sight for sore eyes—even in her waffle long underwear and cutoff army pants. As she hugs me, I realize it is the first time anyone has touched me since the last time she hugged me. I smell her slightly magenta hair. The softness of her polar fleece vest reminds me of little chicks about a week after they hatch.

"We're serving baked potatoes and have several Mr. Potato Heads for your entertainment if you don't feel like dancing with us!" adds Rob. He holds up a piece of brown plastic shaped like a potato. Then he reaches down to the pile of small plastic parts on the table and selects the eyes with the big black glasses, a Roman nose, and big red lips. Finally, he tops the potato with the yellow Cuban-style hat. I think I may have gotten a Mr. Potato Head for my sixth birthday.

"Hey, bro," Paul shouts as he reaches for the sliding glass door in the back of the house. Through the ends of his long nasty dreadlocks I can see he's holding a bong and a Mr. Potato Head. "They've finally progressed beyond disco and into New Wave." He rolls his eyes through his large Coke-bottle glasses. "I'll just be out here." He walks out onto the back porch in his clashing plaid flannel shirt and boxers, rag wool socks, and sheepskin slippers.

Rob is wearing a silky polyester shirt with a seventies psychedelic print of topless women all over it. It shines like his freshly shaven head.

"Nice shirt. Is that new?" I ask.

"Minda bought it for me at the Salvation Army. Other gay guys dig it."

Minda dances past the pile of home brew equipment and into the kitchen while Devo sings "Whip It." She tosses a hot baked potato at me from across the kitchen, still dancing.

"You didn't cook this in the microwave, did you?" I ask. Our microwave—well, our whole kitchen, really—is disgusting because no one ever cleans it. We've had the same sticky yellow fly tape up for about three years now, long covered with fossilized flies. The wall above the stove has a good half-inch coating of bacon grease on it from all the nights Paul gets the munchies and cooks bacon at 3 a.m. We all fear the refrigerator and have stopped using it altogether. Rob duct-taped it shut to protect any of our guests who might dare to open it—as if we ever have guests: No one else can stand the smell in here.

"You know what the microwave reminds me of?" Rob asks. "Those magic rocks we used to put in a glass of water and they grew into colorful stalagmites. Did you have those when you were a kid? I call it 'the magic rocks microwave.' "

"No. Oven-baked, hermetically sealed in tinfoil," Minda assures me in regard to whether the potato was cooked in the microwave. The oven is the one part of the kitchen that is relatively safe due to high temperatures.

"When do you leave?" I ask.

"Two weeks," Minda answers. "Got a bunch of richies from Texas coming in three weeks. Gotta get things ready. Herb and I explored some new mountains in the chopper today. Had to find a baby mountain so the Texans wouldn't hurt themselves but could still go home and tell their friends that they heli-skied Alaska."

"Right." I take a bite of my potato as if it were an apple. "Rob, good season?" I ask.

"Sure. I love being yelled at by the newly married and nearly buried on the Love Boat. And you? Any gunfights at Copper River this year?"

"Oh, you know that's a given," I answer.

I take a Mr. Potato Head and slip out the sliding glass door. I join Paul on the back porch where seven large Hefty bags of garbage have accumulated since someone forgot to pay the garbage bill. Paul likes to sit out here and ponder his mortality while he smokes a bowl, shakes the mice out of the garbage bags, and watches Lavern, the neighbor's gray cat, eat them.

"I see Lavern is glad to have you home," I say.

"We have a special bond based on our mutual fascination with mouse mortality. Good season?" he asks as we explore the various identities of our Mr. Potato Heads.

"Yeah, you know. Fine," I answer. "What about you? Stay off the rocks this year?"

"No. And then we had a little fire in the hull in the middle of the night. Yeah, bro, I was on the national news being airlifted off the boat wearing nothing but boxers and boots. I think the only reason we made national news was that we took aboard that black lab on the dock—you know, the one no one knows who it belongs to—and when the engine exploded, she ran down and hid in the cabin. I ran down and got her, so she was airlifted out, too. The media love a good dog rescue. Some TV guys are going to do a reenactment of it on some *Amazing Rescues* show. I told him I should have monster dreads and be wearing nothing but boots and boxers when the coast guard arrives."

"You're famous," I say.

"As you can tell by all my groupies," he says, gesturing to the large crowds of women that aren't there. He takes another hit off his bong. "Bro, tonight we tap the spruce brew."

"I totally forgot about the spruce brew. It's been fermenting since early May. It must be over 150 proof by now."

"Alaska White Lightning. Minda made Jell-O shooters out of our blackberry brew. A little treat for later."

"Nah, that's just wrong," I say. I get up and sneak past the dancers and into the bathroom I use as a darkroom.

I finish developing the two rolls of film I shot during the summer. When they dry, I put them in envelopes in my file of hundreds of rolls I've shot and developed but haven't printed.

When I come out, Minda and Rob are still dancing. I look through my lens and snap them.

MARA

My first day at work is an orientation day complete with a pot-luck lunch. If there is one thing I detest about being a teacher, it's all the potlucks. In the first place, I don't want to eat what most people eat. I have no interest in eating mayonnaise-based foods or hamburger casseroles made with cream of mushroom soup and crushed potato chips sprinkled on top, and I am not remotely tempted by any dessert made with Cool Whip. Yuck. And, surprise, no one there wants to eat what I eat, either, so there's really no point in making some nice whole-grain veg-etarian dish.

But since I'm homeless right now, I couldn't make a dish if I wanted to.

I go to the store to see what I can bring. Every bachelor in the district will bring chips, so I can't bring those. That's inher-ent sexism in potlucks. I just cringe when a male superinten-dent or principal proposes a potluck. A potluck isn't more work for him or any of the men in the district; a potluck is more work for the women in the district and for the wives of the men in the district. I want to say, Guess what, pal? Just because I have boobs doesn't mean I want to cook for you.

I pick up a watermelon to bring as my contribution, and for my lunch, since I won't be eating anything there, a container of yogurt, some nuts, and an apple. Then I drive to the high school's multipurpose room.

I sit quietly and feel out of place while other teachers around me catch up with each other about their summers. I think most people are teachers because they liked school. I'm a teacher because I didn't. I think this is at the root of why I feel like a foreigner in a crowd of them.

After the potluck we are set free to set up our classrooms. I start with my high school room since I'm already in the high school. I sort through chemicals used in glazes and look for firing cones in the cluttered cupboards. I dump water in the clay bin, knowing it will never soften before tomorrow. I discover there is no blue watercolor paint left anywhere. I find a lot of charcoal and newsprint. I guess I'll start with that. Drawing is a good place to start.

Then I drive to the elementary school and explore the art room there. I immediately love it because it's old and at one time it was clearly a K-12 school. There is a broken kiln, some photography equipment I don't know what to do with, and a fifty-year supply of tempura paint. Every cupboard is like an archaeological dig, telling the story of the last sixty years in that building.

The next day the kids come. My day starts off with half-hour blocks at the elementary school, starting with the difficult and self-conscious sixth and fifth graders, progressing to the curious and willing fourth and third graders, and ending with the excited and enthusiastic little ones. I start the year off with a lesson about the first art element, line, and the fourth art element, color, by putting on different kinds of music and inviting students to make different kinds of lines in different colors that interpret that music. I do it with them, and some imitate me. This is all right because they're learning to think differently, and sometimes you have to imitate at first while you think about why you're doing what you're doing or consider other ways to do it. The kindergartners are the most fun because even though many of them just make random scribbles that look the same on every paper for the different kinds of music, I know they understand the idea because some of them can't contain their excitement and end up interpreting through dance or movement what I had invited them to show me on paper.

Manuel is the only Hispanic student in the whole school, but he's confident and proud and the leader of the dancing. During "Flight of the Bumblebee," he scoots around the room in urgent and frantic shuffles. A few join while others watch, scribble, and giggle. During the music of Nusrat Fateh Ali Khan, Manuel makes his arms curve, spiral, and undulate. I smile widely in delight at how well he interprets music. During Bob Marley, he bounces in exaggerated up-and-down movements, and, finally, during Miles Davis, he makes every movement as big and excited as he can. He's joyous. I think about the inhibited and sulky sixth graders and wonder what happens to us and why. When do we lose that joy or at least learn to temper it?

At lunch I drive to the high school. My fifth-period class, the one that immediately follows lunch, has a wide assortment of kids in it, from the cowboy and the good girls to the two severe-looking, almost punk rock girls and the group of boys who appear to be stoned out of their gourds. I introduce myself, hand out my syllabus, go over safety rules, and ask them what in particular they'd like to learn about or experience in my class. No one raises their hand and no one talks. It's creepy.

I noticed it when they first came in. They didn't talk even to each other. I don't know if it's because they're uncomfortable with me or with each other—if it's a Wild Kingdom thing, like a bunch of wild animals thrown into a cage together who won't be comfortable until they sort out what the pecking order is, whose territory is whose, and perhaps even who will be getting devoured. In the end I ask them to put on paper what they're interested in learning. Most of them don't even look at me.

My sixth-period class is the opposite, but not necessarily in a positive way. They're loud. Two students boisterously exchange tips on hiding drugs from the drug dog. (In the light fixture was their favorite.) Their language is inappropriate when they talk with one another about their summer. Finally, the bell rings. When I ask this group what they want to learn, I'm met with blank stares.

After a long, awkward silence, Tara raises her hand. "Most people are in this class because there was nowhere else for us to go."

This is my at-risk group that no one warned me about. One wrong move in one direction, and they'll disengage. One wrong move in the other direction, and they'll devour me. As I introduce myself and go over my positive expectations, I make eye contact with each one of them, and each one of them looks me in the eye. That's what I like about naughty kids. They've got gumption like that. And because I'm new and they haven't been rude to me yet, I know I have the opportunity to be the first teacher to ever tell them that even though they might be here because they had nowhere else to go, I'm really glad they're here because I can look in their eyes and tell they have all kinds of things to say, opinions to express, and stories to tell. And I look forward to seeing how they'll tell those things through their art. They exchange sideways looks at each other like they want to laugh at me, and that's okay with me today. I know they don't want the others to see that maybe they might actually be excited about something.

One girl doesn't exchange glances with the others, and she doesn't smile. When I look at her, she looks angrily back. She looks like a smaller, younger me, but with hair a much brighter shade of red and brown eyes instead of green. She's much shorter than I am, too. When I call out roll, I learn her name is Kelli.

Finally, my seventh-period class is gregarious and fun. They smile. They joke. They ask questions about how to get an A. They get along. It's a huge class, but there's no tension in it. I look around and wonder why. Several of my students are girl athletes. There are more underclassmen in this class, but the seniors who are in it are the student government types who care about winning scholarships. I can see in their eyes that while they have the normal level of small-town angst, they're hungry for a bigger world and determined to work for the opportunity to get there. Because of these seniors, the younger kids don't have to act out to win the older kids' respect. I can tell this class is going to be a part of my day I look forward to. "Kevin, Nate, Emily, Brent, Cara, Kate, Elle," I call out. Yeah, I'm going to like this class. There's something special about this class.

❧

When Earl told me I could fix up this place any way I saw fit, I knew he expected me to fix the stairs and the roof, but I don't think he expected all this. I painted a mural of a giant dog on the side of the small outbuilding. It's a dog that has been traveling with me in my lucid dreams lately; he's a Samoyed mix of some kind with little white spots over his eyes like eyebrows and a bottom tooth missing that shows when he smiles. My stained glass is up in the windows, of course. I am in the process of adding a greenhouse onto the other side of the little house, but since I'm accumulating windows from thrift stores, it's going to take me a while to finish. But I did build a brick oven outside from the pile of bricks where another ranch house used to sit. I must tell you, there is nothing like bread baked in a brick oven. The biggest change is undoubtedly what I did to the entryway. I busted out the old entry and rebuilt it in a way that sort of looks like an old church tower except smaller. Instead of having a bell in the tower, I hung several wind chimes so that my new house sounds like an Indonesian gamelan concert.

The McRaes call my house the Church of the Dog, which I find very funny.

I've created flower boxes and garden spaces, although all that is in them right now are bulbs in cages (so the rodents don't get them). Bulbs and compost. I'm in heaven with all this abundant compost material.

Using rotted fence posts, I've started some dog sculptures in the yard around the house. I don't know how long they'll last. Maybe I'll try to build a little foundry at some point and cast them in iron.

Lately I've just been drawn to the dogs as a symbol of the divine protective spirit. I guess it's the dog in my dream that has gotten me thinking about it.

Earl and I spend our Saturdays fixing fences. Well, first he goes to the local café to meet with his friends for coffee, and I go make waffles for Edith and me. I figure after sixty years of cooking for other people, it might be nice to have someone cook for you, and, well, I like to eat with other people once in a while. Then Earl comes home, and we go fix fences.

Earl teaches me about ranch life and tells me where summer and winter ranges are for the deer, where animals can find water when, what the presence of different birds acting in different ways means, and how to predict the weather.

Harvey, the hog, follows us all over the ranch on Saturdays. Earl gives me all kinds of grief about the practicality of feeding a hog I'm never going to eat, but I tell him it's really no different than a dog and is perhaps more practical because hogs eat more of my vegetarian table scraps. Of course this opens up yet another can of worms.

No topic is a safe one with Earl. Ever since he saw the big metal Craftsman toolbox that Dad gave me for Christmas when I turned fourteen, the year he died, Earl and I spend much of our time having lengthy debates over tools: Stanley versus Craftsman; whether cordless screwdrivers are a blessing or a curse; when a socket is better than a wrench; and the problem that metrics have caused: "Now you got to have two different wrench and socket sets!" This last topic usually leads to the sore topic of my pickup and the importance of buying American.

Every Saturday morning he has a big bump on the side of his neck, and while he talks at me about the evils of my pickup and I try in vain to convince him that some Toyotas are made in the United States and that parts for Ford are made overseas now, I send in a narrow beam of red laser energy—sort of liquid light if you can imagine that—to blow up that bump cell by cell. By Sunday morning it's smaller, but by the following Saturday, it's back up to its previous size.

All I'm doing is buying him a little more time to put his life in order, I guess, although since none of us get off this planet alive, buying more time on this planet is really all "saving" is, anyway. Healing is another matter. Healing is something you have to do for yourself. Healing is what happens to your soul, to your life, to your relationships with others. Healing does not always extend the length of your time on this planet, but healing is all that truly matters.

Today we got back just before a lightning storm began to

rip. I do not like lightning. I acknowledge it as part of the balance of our living planet. If you think about it, the atmosphere is like the planet's aura, and in that light what goes on in the planet's energy field is intriguing to me. But in another light it just scares the hell out of me. I guess because I know I have a bigger energy field than most people, and it stands to reason that lightning would be more attracted to me than even metallic objects. But Gram taught me "what you give your attention to grows," so I try not to give my attention to getting fried by a bolt of lightning.

Outside my window, I hear a whimper.

I open the door to find the dog from my dreams that I painted on my house standing in the rain. The rain rolls off his white and gray fur. I don't really know how this all works—you know, like where he came from exactly . . . what dimension. And I don't really know why he travels in my dreams with me. It could be that in my dreams I traveled to the future. Or it could also be that I was out in some dimensions where God thought it might be better if I had a protective spirit with me, and then figured I could use his services here on Earth, too. I don't know. Maybe dogs are teachers. Maybe they are sent to us from Heaven to teach us how to be protective Guardian Angels for each other here on Earth.

Whatever the case may be, I figure what else can you name your soul dog who appears to you on a night with lightning besides Zeus?

I open the door and let Zeus in. He lies next to my short futon bed, and I am thankful to have a protective spirit to put my arm around on this terrifying night as I fall asleep.

AUTUMN

🐕

DANIEL

From my darkroom I can hear Minda call a bear alert to Rob. We were thinking we might have to break down and do something about all the Hefty bags of garbage on our back porch that attract all kinds of wildlife, and then we discovered that Rob could scare away darn near anything by singing almost any Bee Gees song at them. In the moments that follow I hear the back door open, Rob wail out the first two lines of "Stayin' Alive," and then a victorious cheer from Minda and Paul.

I finish developing a roll of film that I took of Minda, Rob, and Paul in our daily life here at the house. I just stick the negatives in an envelope and tuck it away. It's nice to know I can always pull the negatives out and print pictures if I ever need to remember something.

When I come out, Minda, Rob, and Paul are decorating the Christmas tree from last year that's been sitting on the back porch since they took it out sometime around Valentine's Day. They brought it in, and instead of putting it in a stand, they just leaned it up against the wall in the corner of the room. They pass Paul's brownies and decorate the tree with Minda's extensive Pez dispenser collection. Tonight's musical selection is "Feed the World" or whatever that song from the eighties is where the proceeds were supposed to help starving people in Ethiopia. Their task at hand is momentarily interrupted when Rob makes the Wonder Woman Pez tell the Darth Vader Pez that she could kick his ass and that he really needs a makeover. This launches them into a debate as to whose ass Wonder

Woman really could kick and ultimately who is a greater force to be reckoned with: Wonder Woman or the Bionic Woman.

I miss their conclusion as I slip out the door to the backyard where I keep an ice chest hanging from a tree. The cold night smacks my face. Feels like snow. I double-check for bears before I lower the ice chest, remove some smoked salmon, hang it up again, and slip back into the warmth of the foul-smelling house.

"Hey, wanna put towels around our necks like superhero capes and run around the house?" Rob tries to get the others excited about his idea.

"Daniel," Minda says, noticing me. She walks over and puts her arms around my neck. "My little hermit friend. Tomorrow I leave for the heli-ski lodge." Then she begins to sing "I'm so glad we had this time together" from the Carol Burnett show but gets mixed up and ends up singing the song that Mr. Rogers sings at the end of his show. "My little hermit friend, would you like some Jell-O I made with your blackberry brew?"

"Yum. There's always room for Jell-O," Paul says, nodding with a smile, trying to persuade me to go for it. "You guys," he says as he takes another handful of Jell-O, "this is the best Christmas I've ever had."

It's only September, but I let it slide and enjoy a little Jell-O with my smoked salmon.

ᙏᐱᖇᐱ

As I walk into the high school during lunch, I reflect on what a bizarre and illogical career choice I've made since I hated high school so much the first time around. When I walk down the hall, I have to remind myself that I'm no longer a powerless misfit teenager and that no one is going to hurt or threaten me.

I remember being fifteen, dressed in mostly black with a short spiked hairdo and wearing boots that looked like wrestling shoes. A group of fifteen guys surrounded me on the edge of campus. They were loggers' kids and meaner than anything found west of coal country.

"Nice boots," one said sarcastically.

"Thanks," I said back, like I didn't get the sarcasm.

"Where'd you get 'em? Goodwill?" another said.

"Yup," I replied even though I didn't. I kept my cool, knowing the minute they saw fear, their games would really begin. I kept walking toward campus, with their challenging inbred faces in my face. Inside my pocket I gripped my knife, which I hoped I wouldn't have to use.

Just then a teacher walked out of his room, and the pack of bullies walked off in another direction. But before they disappeared one yelled something back at me that I'd rather not repeat. Even though their words had the power to make me feel sexually violated, physically I wasn't. I was safe again for the moment. I went to the music room and took my bass into a tiny practice room where I started to shake and cry, releasing the fear and stress of just another daily incident.

Sometimes I wonder now why I made it so difficult for myself. Why didn't I just wear the same thing everyone else wore? Why didn't I just grow my hair and slip under the radar? I had just lost my father. I really didn't need any more heartache. I guess, in retrospect, I was angry—so angry that I didn't know what to do. Maybe all that black and that spiky hair was the only way I could express my depression and anger without hurting other people. I don't know. Maybe everyone's teenage years are an era of temporary insanity.

That would explain why teaching high school requires acting more like a police officer, something I never had any desire to do. I hate this role. I feel boxed in. I spend the day wanting to scream, "I don't want to be a public school teacher! I want to be the wild woman I truly am!" But I don't scream.

I wait until after school, and find an old dirt road where motor vehicles are supposedly not allowed. As I get away from the main road, I lose my restrictive clothes and just enjoy feeling free. Nothing sexual about it. I just can't wear my teacher costume for one more minute. And after a couple of miles I start to feel more like myself.

℀

The next day when the students enter my class, I know from looking at their auras that something is not right. They look darker, and the more joyous colors, like the yellows and turquoises, are missing. Some have visible leaks where the rainbow spills out of the normal egg-shaped sphere.

I listen to their conversations carefully and put together that most had been watching the U.S. bomb Iraq on the TV in other classrooms. There is a chemical weapon storage facility nearby, and I can tell this weighs heavily on their minds. They speculate about whether or not Three Hills would be a target. They ask me lots of questions, most of which I don't know the answer to, including one about the location of the bomb shelter. I just reply that personally I'd rather die than be locked in a basement with a couple hundred teenagers and no bathrooms.

I feel my energy drain, too. It's almost like there's this black hole created by fear that sucks all our spirits in, even those of us who do not believe we are in any danger at all. What people don't understand is that thoughts have energetic reality. I watch their fearful thoughts come out of their heads, float around as black bubbles, and land on other people. Energetically, it's like being in a room with twenty people puking on you. Everyone, including me, gets completely covered in negative thought-form vomit. I feel myself get weaker and weaker, and slide into a chair before I fall.

When class ends, I go into the little office part of my room, shut the door and the blinds, and lose it—or release it, depending on how you want to look at it. I'm rattled for so many reasons. Certainly the psychic pollution is a huge factor, but so is the sense that a scab had been picked in the part of the world where my father had fallen in combat. And it has something to do with being unexpectedly put into the position where I am asked to explain the very darkest acts of humankind. It has something to do with being asked what kind of a world we live in. Even though this picture of the world we live in as seen on CNN during bombing coverage is not the whole picture, in the moment it seemed like it, and I didn't have an answer for them.

At first I'm reluctant to leave my office, knowing my emotions, so close to the surface, are obvious to anyone. But then I think to myself, I am a woman, and thank God for me. Why should I be ashamed that it hurts me to watch children in fear? I walk out of school with my eyes bloodshot, my skin blotchy, my nose red, and my head up. I am a woman. I care deeply about children. I will not apologize for that, and I will not hide it to make others more comfortable. I am a woman, and I have a different truth to broadcast.

I wonder when honoring our truth became a sign of weakness, and I feel for all the women before me who were patronized for broadcasting their emotional truth.

I go to the phone booth outside the front of the school and call Gram. "Hi," I try to say cheerfully when she answers.

"You've been watching the news, haven't you?" she asks accusingly yet compassionately. I never could fool her into thinking everything was okay when it was not. "You know better than to watch the news, honey."

"Gram, just remind me about how everything is in divine order?"

"Everything is in divine order."

"And how really there is no right or wrong?" I sound pathetic.

"There is no right or wrong. There is no good or bad. Everything simply is."

"Thanks, Gram."

That night Gram shows up in my dream at my house. "I thought maybe you could use a little vacation," she explains. "How about tonight we go somewhere you want to go?"

The next thing I know, we are praying in a Nepalese Buddhist monastery. The monks look up and smile at us, and we smile back.

DANIEL

Dear Daniel,

I'm not young anymore, and you'll be inheriting the ranch before you know it. Some girl has fixed all your fences for you. Be sure to thank her. Allow her and her pet hog to live on the ranch in her Church of the Dog—you'll understand when you see it—for as long as she likes. Please consider spending this winter with us.

Love,

Grandpa Earl

Another request. And this time he said please.

The first snow. The first snow of every year haunts me. I sit in front of the window at dusk and watch the heavy flakes float down. I remember how the thick flakes hit the windshield of my dad's pickup and splattered in a way that reminded me of crocheted blankets the old women sold at church bazaars. It was one of my last thoughts before we all went over the edge.

I hate the first snow each year. I shake my head to break free from the memories in the window and go help myself to a drink of what was supposed to be spruce beer even though I swore I wouldn't drink that shit.

Then, with my cup in hand, I surrender to the snow and walk into the night wishing that by virtue of the same weather I could cross the line to where my parents live.

The snow silences the town. That's another reason I hate snow. Snow is so very silent. It doesn't splash like water. I focus on the sound of my boots' soles squeaking in the dry snow. The sound keeps me sane.

I make my way back to the house, grab Lavern, and take her in my room with me so I can listen to her breathe as I fall asleep.

A woman with long golden red hair, glowing white skin, and a sheer, short, white dress sits on the back of a white horse that has white feathers hanging in its long mane. "You really need to come home," she says to me.

"What?" I say.

"You really need to come home," she says again.

"Why?" I ask.

"Just do it."

"I don't want to go home," I say.

"You really need to come home. Come on," she says firmly.

I stand on my bed in my boxer shorts while the woman rides the horse alongside my bed. I hold on to her shoulder, slide a leg over the horse, and sit behind her. She turns the horse and begins to walk.

My eyes fly open, and I bolt upright out of a dead sleep. I sit up in bed for a minute, take a couple deep breaths, rub my eyes, and then lie down again, but I don't sleep. I stare at the ceiling and think that maybe I really do need to go home.

From Valdez I drive up through Keystone Canyon. The dusting of snow we received last night melts off, revealing the autumn colors that dot the lush canyon. The canyon narrows as I continue to drive up. No matter how many times I drive through, I never get tired of all the waterfalls.

Everything opens up at the top of Thompson Pass. I pull over and stare at the endless mountaintops.

I cross the border and enter Canada. I stop in Haines Junction for the night and get a room in a cheap dive.

The next morning I gas up and continue on Highway 1 until it's time to turn down the Cassiar Highway, notoriously narrow and windy and in a constant state of construction that leaves numerous twenty-mile stretches of dirt between here and there.

Bears, mostly blacks, like to graze on the side of the road where it's open and easier to walk, and where food is plentiful. Occasionally I have to brake to avoid one in the road, but usually I just have to brake for RVs.

If I had a dollar for every time I drove over a rise to find a damned RV parked in the middle of the road watching a moose, I could take Minda, Paul, and Rob out for a good steak at The Pipeline.

RVs also suck up all the gas so that it's not uncommon for the rest of us to pull into a town and find they're out. If you never let your tank get below half, sometimes you can make it the next hundred and fifty miles to the next town with a gas station. Today I reach Dease Lake only to find that two of the three gas stations have signs saying they are out of gas, and the third has a sign saying they will be back in a half hour. Five hours later they return, and I finally get to fill up along with the others who have been waiting. I continue on, and I curse every RV on the road. Bastards.

I stay in Bell II my second night. It's been turned into a luxurious heli-ski lodge since the last time I drove through.

On day three I reach Highway 97 at Prince George, and the road finally straightens out a little. I stay on it until I reach Kamloops, where I spend my third night. The land around me starts to feel more like home. Tumbleweeds float across the road in the wind.

Finally, on day four, I reach the U.S. border. I drive through Washington State all the way to the Columbia River Gorge. I cross the bridge by McNary Dam and enter Oregon. Finally, Highway 207 takes me all the way back to where I was born.

I feel like a salmon. Salmon swim to the sea when they are young, feed and grow for several years, and get fat. Then they stop eating and begin their journey up the freshwater to their inland birthplaces. They jump anything in their path, determined to go home. I wish I felt that level of determination, but I don't. I just sat for three and a half days with my foot on the gas pedal. I guess that's where the comparison ends.

Once salmon get home, they mate and die. The odds of me mating in Three Hills are slim to none. As for the dying, there is a part of me that feels like it's dying as I return here. But I'm only staying for a week or so. And most of the time I feel ambivalent about my life anyway.

It's like I'm watching a movie. I'm in the movie, but I'm just sort of a character I don't care about in a movie I don't care about. As I watch myself interact with other people in the movie, I don't really feel anything. I don't really feel anything at all.

MARA

In my dream I'm looking for someone, anyone, to teach me to waltz. I'm walking all over the downtown area of my hometown looking for assistance. I feel an urgency about learning. A song by the Innocence Mission, "My Waltzing Days Are Over," follows me everywhere I go.

Two different people try to help—one a ranger I knew when I worked in the Olympic Rain Forest, and the other a woman I've never met.

Each leads me in an attempt to teach me, but they do not have enough clarity in the way they move to resolve the question nagging at me. Neither has a verbal answer when I articulate my waltz question, either. I continue to search for someone to dance with me.

See, I could be confused, but I have it in my mind that a waltz goes slow-slow-quick-quick, and each measure is supposed to start with a new foot. I have figured out, though, that if your second quick is a full step, your weight is on the foot that you are supposed to take your next slow with. Based on this, I figure waltzes are either truly slow-slow-quick-quick-quick, a triplet, or slow-slow-quick-pause. The question nags at me.

DANIEL

I take a moment and survey the ranch. The arena where I used to practice riding bulls in front of Grandpa and Whitey is all overgrown now. The window in the shed I knocked out with a baseball is still broken. A couple pieces of roofing are missing from the barn. Hopefully, Grandpa will get that woman he wrote about up there to fix it instead of me. God, how I hate heights. They remind me of the accident. Raspberry bushes completely cover the old outhouse that no one ever used in my lifetime. Grandma's horse, Winter, nickers at me from the corral. Buck, the sadistic buckskin that used to charge me when I was a boy, is now gone from the herd.

Grandpa comes out to greet me, enthusiastically patting me on the back. "Welcome home," he says, and something about the word *home* leaves me feeling heavy. I wish I could feel as happy to see Grandpa as he is to see me, and as happy to be home as he is happy to have me home, but I don't.

"I see Buck's gone," I say to change the subject.

"Yeah. I knew you were going to miss him." Grandpa laughs.

"About as much as I miss a bad cold," I reply with a courtesy laugh.

"I think Buck launched you clear out of the Earth's atmosphere that last time, didn't he? You needed one of them spacesuits for that launch." He pats my shoulder. "Hey, Hank and Whitey are coming out the Saturday after next to help bring in the steers. You're just in time. Mara will be riding, too." He gestures over toward the building with the dog on it. "Though she claims to have an ethical conflict over it. She's one of them vegetarians. You'll meet her later. She's at school now."

I pause to look at her place. "Wow, that is really something."

"Yeah, we call it the Church of the Dog. Get this. She paints a giant picture of a dog on the side, and then maybe two weeks later a real dog that looks just like it shows up at her door during a thunderstorm." Grandpa makes Twilight Zone noises. "You'll see him around. Zeus. He's a good dog."

"Huh. That must be the pet hog?" I gesture toward the pen.

"Yeah, the McDougal kid got a little hysterical at the county fair 4-H auction. Put an EAT BEEF sign on him. Since Mara's one of them vegetarians, you can pretty much guess the rest of that story."

I laugh. Grandpa really seems excited about all the new additions to the ranch.

"See that?" Grandpa points to the roof problem on the barn. "I saved that just for you."

"Oh, goody. You know how I love heights," I say.

Then I hear Grandma's voice. "Oh, my land! Earl, who is this handsome stranger in our backyard? Get in here! I'll make you a turkey sandwich! I made an apple pie just this morning! I had a feeling it was going to be a special day!"

"Come on, boy. Let's go strap on the feed bag," Grandpa says. He pats my shoulder again as we walk into the house.

❧

I drop my bag off in my old bedroom, which hasn't changed since I was a kid. My old bull-riding trophies cover the dresser, and ribbons hang from nails on the wall. I stop to study a newspaper picture of me and Tim holding up trophies. Several other newspaper pictures of me are taped to the edges of the mirror above the dresser.

I remember riding bulls as if I were riding in slow motion. The twisting and thrashing. My teenage body being whipped around like a rag doll despite my attempts to master control within chaos. Being spiked to the ground like a volleyball and running wildly to the fence to escape the horns behind me. And I remember feeling very separate from everyone else as I clung to the fence until the bull trotted out of the arena: me looking up at the crowd of smiling people and wondering what it feels like to be them, wondering if they really were as happy as they seem or if they felt as disconnected from everyone as I did but just hid it better.

Regardless of whether I made my eight seconds or not, Grandpa and Whitey would be standing together cheering. Then Whitey would work his way down to the chutes to give me pointers to help me on my next go-around.

Grandma would never go. She said it was enough to lose her kids; she didn't need to watch her only grandson get killed, too. It was a point of contention between Grandma and Grandpa. His pride and her fear.

When I was twenty, I qualified for the circuit finals in Pendleton, which is a pretty big deal. Grandpa was out of his mind with pride. He had Whitey over several times a week to watch videotapes of the rodeos that had been on that week so he could point out the finer points of bull riding to me.

I can't remember why I was late that day. I just remember the moment I realized that if I wanted to get there on time, I couldn't take the long loop through Echo. I'd have to take the road my parents died on. I realized how humiliated Grandpa would be when I wasn't there on time, but I couldn't make myself drive the road. I started driving toward Echo to give myself a chance in case I thought of an alternative that would get me there on time, but in the end I realized it was hopeless. So instead of turning off to Echo, I just kept driving north until I reached Valdez where I wouldn't have to face anyone, and I never returned. I got a job on a salmon boat and floated away.

EDITH

I hear a knock at the back door, but before I can answer it, Daniel does. I watch their awkward introduction as I walk in.

"Hi, I'm Daniel."

"Mara."

They shake hands. He ducks his head. "I've got to go . . . uh . . ." He points up the stairs. "You know, unpack."

"Oh, okay," I say, disappointed. I wish I had done a better job of teaching him basic social skills. He makes his escape.

"Edith, I dreamt about waltzing the other night. I couldn't get anyone to tell me whether it goes slow-slow-quick-quick, which would start me off on the wrong foot for the next measure, or whether it's slow-slow-quick-quick-quick. Can you tell me?" Mara asks at my back door.

"Earl! Will you teach Mara to dance!"

Earl gets out of his easy chair in the other room and walks over to us. He looks at Mara for a minute while he decides. "I guess," he resigns.

I sit down at the piano and play a waltz.

"What are we doing?" Mara asks.

"You're following me," Earl answers.

"Yeah, but what are we doing?" she asks again.

"Don't worry about it. All you have to do is follow." Earl steps all over her toes. "So this is the real reason you're not married!

"Excuse me?" she asks

"You can't court without waltzing!" he exclaims. Then he adds, "How do you think I wooed Edith? With my charm?"

"What charm?" I call out.

Mara laughs.

This takes me back to my first dance with Earl. He made my whole spine tingle. He was the handsomest young man in the county and by far the best dancer. I had wild roses braided in my hair. I noticed how he tried to get a whiff of my roses without getting inappropriately close to me. Catching glimpses of his temptation made me feel delicious. I've never felt more beautiful in my life than I did that night. I felt like a flower myself. He was the sun that made me bloom.

He was a different man then. Losing a child changes people. I sometimes think it's worse for men, because they don't cry—the ones from my generation don't anyway. All those tears of grief just sit in their hearts and rot.

Speaking of grief, now he's saying, "You're not married because you need to learn to follow. And you're not putting any effort into finding a man. Why aren't you looking for a man?"

"Looking for a man for what?" she asks.

"To marry."

"Oh, gee, Earl," she stammers nervously for a minute. "I just barely escaped marriage. I was engaged to a man who tried to break my spirit. I think I'd rather go through life solo than go through that again, if you don't mind." All the while she beams up at him with love in her eyes, like she would look at a grandpa.

"Edith, did I break your spirit?" he asks me facetiously.

"Not yet!" I call back to them with all the spunk I can muster.

"He divided all the bills every week, split them exactly in two, and billed me at the end of the week. He charged me ten bucks for a trip to the hospital once," she explains.

"What kind of man does that?" I ask.

"Men didn't used to do that. I think they're confused by all you women acting like men," Earl says as they continue to dance.

"What are you talking about?" Mara asks, incredulous.

"Yeah, hardly any women stay home and keep the house anymore. How are the men supposed to do all the things men do when women are already doing them?" Earl asks.

"Earl, maybe women have had to do that because the divorce rate is so high and so many women are raising children on their own," she answers.

"Maybe the divorce rate is so high because none of you know how to cook," he says.

Mara laughs. "Yeah, that's probably it. How simple! Or maybe it's because none of them know how to cook."

"Do you want a husband or a wife?" he asks.

"I just want my dog," she says, getting better at following his steps.

"You really should open your mind," I say.

"Even in times of extreme desperation, Edith, I still have one standard: no chewing tobacco. Fortunately, that standard has ruled out all the single men in a four-county radius and has saved me a lot of trouble."

The house seems warm and full tonight. For too long this house has had only the two of us in it, not a family. Such a huge house for just two people. For decades this house has felt as empty as my heart after the kids died. But tonight the room seems to glow with joy as I try to reconcile the bittersweet conflict of a perfect moment—that is, enjoying the perfection, yet knowing it's not the nature of these moments to last. Perfect moments make me realize how fragile my life is, along with everything in it.

Finally Earl says, "All right. You're a pro waltzer now. You're ready to be courted. Come back next week for the fox-trot."

As we walk her to the door, I hear the squeaky stair and figure Daniel was probably hiding on those stairs, peeking around the corner, and secretly watching the whole lesson. If I had a dollar for every time I heard that stair squeak during important conversations, especially when we had company, I'd be a rich woman.

"Thanks, Earl. Thanks, Edith. Good night!" Mara sings out as she walks out the back door.

"Good night, dear!" I call out to her.

I go back to the living room put on an old record of dance songs, and then go upstairs where I pluck wild roses out of the dried flower bouquet that sits on my bureau. I had dried them last spring, and now I stick them in my hair and return downstairs to Earl.

He understands, and we dance close. He sticks his nose in my hair while we waltz and waltz. And for the next forty minutes I feel as delicious as I did sixty-one years ago.

"I don't tell you enough how much I love you," he says.

"I know you love me," I reply.

"No, there's no way you could possibly know how much you mean to me. I should've been tellin' you, showin' you for years." His hand slips more firmly onto the small of my back, and he gives me the most loving kiss I have ever known. Tears stream down my cheeks.

DANIEL

Before I go to bed, Grandpa knocks on my open door. "I . . . I . . ." Grandpa stammers. "Um, I . . . I just wanted to say how nice it is you're here," he manages to get out, although I don't think it's what he came up here to say. "I . . . um . . ." he starts again. I can tell he's trying really hard to say something. His eyebrows are scrunched together the way they do whenever he's struggling with something. "I . . . I'll see you in the morning."

"Thanks, Grandpa. It's good to be here," I say even though it is really not.

He gives me a smile and a wink and shuts my door. The door shutting was the worst sound in the world to me when I was a boy. And the stillness and silence that would follow took me back to the stillness and silence of my parents' truck. No matter where I looked, no matter whether my eyes were open or closed, I could not stop seeing their bloody lifeless faces.

At once the feeling comes back, and I gasp for breath, trying not to panic more. I run to the window, wrestle with it until it opens, and stick my head out into the air. "It's okay, it's okay, it's okay," I whisper to myself just to hear noise. "It's okay," I whisper until I believe it. But I leave the window open just so I can hear the cattle and the crickets as I try to sleep in this haunted room.

❧

I'm up on the barn roof where I didn't want to be. "I'm gonna stay down here so I can call 911 if you need it!" Grandpa kids me from down below.

"You're too kind!" I shout back.

"Hey, I told Whitey you'd go over and fix his barn roof when you were done here!"

"You didn't!"

"Okay, I didn't. But I sure had you goin' there for a minute, didn't I?" he responds.

I just laugh and finish tearing out the rotted wood.

As I climb down and land, he puts his hand on my shoulder, still sort of laughing at his own joke. "You know, I don't mean anything by givin' you such a bad time. If I thought you feared the roof like you feared the circuit finals, I wouldn't've put you up there."

It is the first time he's ever brought the finals up since it happened. I look at the ground and quietly say, "I wasn't afraid of the circuit finals, Grandpa. I was late and didn't want to drive the only road that would get me there on time." I don't look up. I just walk toward the barn.

He follows me to where we stand by the pile of dusty old boards wedged against a wall.

"That one will do, and maybe that one, too," I say. Then I dig through the pile.

"Look out for nails," Grandpa says. "Mara got one in her hand when she was building her sauna. Had to get a tetanus shot."

"Hm." I pick up the boards and carry them under my arm to the ladder. Grandpa follows. "Grandpa, I'm sorry I didn't make it to the circuit finals."

"Well, that was a long time ago," he says.

I stop at the ladder, and Grandpa rests his hand on my shoulder for a second before I climb.

"I'm sorry I brought it up," he says.

"Yeah, well, I'm sure you were scared when I didn't show," I say. I begin to replace the rotted wood.

"I drove that road to make sure you weren't in the same spot again."

I wince and stop working. I close my eyes and shake my head regretfully. "I'd give anything to do that day over."

"You never did tell me why you were late," Grandpa says.

"Oh, you know, I was getting in trouble with Tim the night before."

"Oh, yeah? What was her name, and what barn did you wake up in?" He laughs.

"I'll never tell. And yours," I joke back. "Nah, I think Tim drove me home after I passed out. He dumped me in there so I wouldn't get into trouble with you."

"I never did like that kid," he says.

EARL

I sat in the grandstand with Whitey, Owen, and Hank, drinking beer from a plastic cup and watching Clint Waffle make his eight seconds on a Brahma called Hurricane Jack. Good ride. Dan was up next, and my stomach knotted with all the hopes I had for him. The announcer called his name, and I said a silent prayer for his safety as I scanned the chutes for him. My heart sank when the silence lingered and the announcer finally said, "Looks like Daniel McRae isn't going to make it today, folks," and called the next contestant. I excused myself to call home, and when no one answered, my imagination got the best of me. I flashed back to runnin' down that steep slope the kids slid off, past the bumper, past the tailpipe, down the trail of broken glass, answering Daniel's screams, and hopin' that Daniel's bein' alive meant the others were, too. The image of how I found the three of them haunts me. Even after all these years I can't begin to describe it or comprehend it.

I returned home through Echo, the way I knew Daniel would come, scannin' the sides of the roads for his truck or any signs of a recent accident. I made it home without findin' a single fresh skid mark. I asked Edith, who was home now, if she knew anything, which she didn't, and then my eyes began to water as I realized he may have taken the road that winds directly to Pendleton, the road the accident happened on.

I hadn't been on that road since the day after the accident. Just drivin' it made me want to upchuck. I took it slow, despite my panic. I stopped at some of the places where the cliffs were so steep that I couldn't see what lay below the road, as I had done some twenty-five years ago. When I stopped at the place where I found the kids, I upchucked right over the edge.

I was relieved and confused when I arrived in Pendleton without findin' anything but an old red Japanese fuel-efficient gumball machine of a car that had been at the bottom of one of those hills. I called to the car, and when no one answered, I studied the tracks and figured the car had gone down before the last rain. I figured I could just call the sheriff later to verify that he knew about it. I had no interest in lookin' in that car.

I figured Daniel must've just froze up and drove off. I kicked myself for not keepin' a closer eye on him that day. I knew Whitey and I could've kept him from blowin' his big chance.

But I had it wrong. And I can't really blame him for not takin' that road.

MARA

Shawn is a seventeen-year-old mother in my class. I think about her life as a woman in the evening, filled with responsibilities beyond my comprehension, yet under the rules and expectations of a child in the day. It seems silly to me that I am supposed to be her teacher when she is, in truth, mine.

To assist her through the intimidation she's feeling from the sculpture assignment, I put a piece of wadded-up newspaper under a slab of clay. It forms a dome shape now, and with that she reluctantly begins to sculpt.

When I check on her next, I see she's made a very primal-looking mask. Maybe it's not a mask; it doesn't have any holes in it. It's a sad face.

"I like it, Shawn!" I tell her. I make it my practice to only say things I mean, so when I give them a compliment, they know I mean it.

"Yeah, me, too," she replies with an uncharacteristic shyness, momentarily dropping the tough-girl act.

After the bisque fire, she glazes it with tobacco brown, red-brown on the lips, and pinkish brown in the eye sockets. I think to myself, She's going to ruin it, but she's approaching it as an experiment. Since I see that as the fundamental mind-set of revolutionary creators of art, I'm not about to squelch it.

A week later, when I unload the kiln from the glaze fire, I discover the glaze did not ruin it at all. Quite the contrary: It looks old and authentic. It looks like timeless sadness.

I see her on her way to another class an hour before her scheduled art time. "Hey!" I call to her. "Your piece is out! It looks awesome! Go check it out!"

She glances back at the class she's supposed to go to, and then with a sparkle in her eye, she slips into the pottery lab of the art room.

When she emerges, she smiles. "I like it."

"I want to show it in the art show. What do you want to call it?"

"Let me think about it."

When the next class arrives, she works at a table with other students. I ask a couple of the others about naming their works, and they easily spit out names. I ask Shawn for a title again, and she once again replies, "Let me think about it."

"Think fast. I'm making tags now," I tell her.

She approaches me maybe two minutes later, looks me in the eye, pauses, and whispers, "Unwanted Face." I nod.

As I begin the mindless task of making labels, I wonder whose. Whose unwanted face? Hers when she was pregnant? Her child's, unwanted by his father? Hers and her child's, unwanted by the community?

ᴇᴅɪᴛʜ

Mara finished her sauna. Actually, it's a small shed with a bench and a tiny tin wood stove. The sauna door has twelve small panes of glass in it, and we so enjoy looking out at the landscape. She made a triangle-shaped stained-glass window above the door, a wild sun, white and yellow marbles set among the triangles in different hues of yellow radiating into a purple background. I do love the gold and violet light rays that stream in.

"Hm," I reply, looking at the floor. Mara has just told me the story of her student, Shawn, and we are talking about women. "'Course, things were different in my day. Women and men had an agreement. Women expected and demanded that men marry them before having sex so that they knew their child would be cared for. People think we held out for moral reasons, but morality follows practicality."

"Hm . . . so you're saying young women essentially need to unionize," Mara clarifies.

I chuckle. "Well, it's hard to demand anyone buy cows when people are giving away free milk," I reply. "Seems like it would be best for the kids."

Mara throws a couple handfuls of water at the stove in the sauna to steam things up. "Double-edged sword for women," she begins. "On one hand, they were materially provided for, so they could full-time parent; on the other hand, it seems many had to tolerate being treated like servants, becoming invisible, or being abused."

"Sure, for some the arrangement didn't work, but for most I think there was mutual appreciation. Men and women did different things. There was no competition. There was appreciation. We had fewer choices, but I think it was easier," I explain.

"Now I guess it's more extreme," she says. "There are more women extremely worse off, and there are more women extremely happier than they would've been in that arrangement. I think in that day I could've never been an artist like I am now.

Babies are so much work. They don't leave room in your life for much else, though from what I observe, you love them so much, you don't mind. . . . I don't know. I don't know what I truly want. I wonder if creating art is really just a pathetic substitute for creating life, you know? All that creative energy cookin' inside me with nowhere to go. Maybe the whole reason I think it's so much more fun to be an artist than a mom is that I've never really allowed myself to think about what it would feel like to be a mom . . . that new level of love other women try to tell you about. On occasion I allow myself to entertain the idea for about five seconds. Then I'm left feeling sad about not being a mom, and it strikes me as so unnatural that I haven't had a child. You know, like what other animal has no offspring nearly twenty years after reaching sexual maturity? And then I feel angry that I'm choosing not to be a mom because if I ever decided to be a mom, I'd probably have to raise that child all by myself. It seems like being a mom should be our biological entitlement, and yet, because it takes so much to attain the standard of living we are expected to have, we have come to see being a full-time mom as a privilege." She suddenly seems self-conscious at having gotten so intense. "So what can you do? Become a teacher and borrow other people's kids." With that she tries to lighten things up.

I don't buy her idea about women today thinking that being a full-time mom is a privilege. "I think women don't want to stay home with babies. I think money is just an excuse. I think the truth is, being a stay-at-home mom is the hardest thing they've ever done, and they want nothing to do with it. They can't get out of their houses fast enough," I declare.

"Do you think respect plays a part in it?" Mara asks. "Do you think moms are less respected now, so working that hard for no respect is contributing to moms not wanting to do it?"

"Hm . . . I don't think it's even recognized what it takes

to raise a child. All these people asking mothers if they work. What is that all about? They have no idea. No recognition, no respect, and no idea," I state.

Mara nods as she thinks. We are quiet for a while, and then she says, "I think I still prefer my choices." There is another pause. "But I do see a lot of others overwhelmed by the same choices and getting lost."

"I guess too many choices or too few choices can make a woman feel lost, depending on the woman," I say, thinking of my friends, some who did have dreams outside of family, dreams they never even dared to tell their husbands about.

"Hm," she says in agreement.

"Just seems like back then mothering was enough. Now no one gives a flying hoot about mothering. All men care about these days is money. They want their women to bring home money."

"Hm . . . somewhere the choice became obligation?" she questions.

"Used to be, we were valued just for being women."

"Do you think women lowered their expectations of men and let them off the hook, or do you think men are just plain dropping the ball?" Then she quickly adds, "Generally speaking, of course, because I do see some really great fathers out there."

"Mm . . . both. You know, 'Why buy the cow if you can milk it for free?' "

"You know, Edith, I don't want to be milked for free, and by that I mean taken advantage of, but I don't want to be bought, either."

I wonder what these young women are so afraid of. I don't really see them getting ahead to anywhere. Most of them just seem tired and lonely. We used to get respect.

ᖱANIEL

The feed lot fences are in need of some serious repair. In a couple weeks about two hundred yearlings will be brought here, weaned, sorted, and fed for two or three months before being sent off to a larger feed lot somewhere else—most of them, anyway. The best-quality third of all the heifers will be kept to replace the old ones that have lost so many teeth that they'll never make it through another winter. As I replace boards, I hear hooves and look up to see a tall, skinny guy who sort of looks like the kid on the cover of *Mad Magazine*, only with a narrower face. It's Tim. The hips of his old bay stick out now.

"Hey! I heard you was back in town!" he shouts as he rides up.

"Word spreads fast!" I answer. "I just got here a couple days ago. Is that your old cutting horse?"

"Yeah, this is Shilo, all right. She's thirty-one now, but she can still buck me off from time to time."

"I'd buck you off, too, if I was an arthritic grandmother and you crawled on my back," I say.

"Nah. She likes it. Gives her a sense of purpose," he says. He ties her to a timber, reaches into his saddlebag, pulls out two cans of Budweiser, and hands one to me.

Out of habit I look back at the house to see if anyone sees me, and then I duck behind the barn with Tim. Our backs slide down the barn wall until we find our seats in the dirt. We carefully crack the explosive beers and slurp.

"So what have you been up to?" I ask.

"Well, I just got back from Moses Lake. I was visiting my son. He's ten now."

"Wait. You have a son?" I ask. "How is that possible? I was there when that bull landed on your nuts."

"I know," he says. "When my son's mother first told me I

had a son—that was just three years ago—I was like, 'No you don't, you golddigger! I know that ain't me! I can't have kids!' I called Doc Anderson just to make sure I had proof if she took me to court, and he says that every once in a great while something like this heals, so I should come in for a test." Tim takes a drink. "Well, he didn't tell me I'd have to . . . you know . . . in a cup. After the first hour . . ."

I start laughing. "The first hour?"

"Yeah, after the first hour, Doc Anderson knocked on the door to ask how things were going, and I was like, 'Doc! I think you just killed any chance I had of giving you anything today!'"

"Isn't Ben's little sister a nurse there now?" I ask.

"Oh, yeah," he says, leaving no question that he thinks she's hot. "But let us not forget that my great-aunt is the receptionist there, and she knows what I'm in the little room for and what I'm supposed to be doing."

"No," I say, horrified for him.

"Yes," he says definitively. "So I finally pick up my cell phone—"

"And what? Call a 1-900 number?" I ask.

"No. I ordered a pizza and a half rack of beer. It finally arrived and that did the trick. After that, I just went . . ." He looks down at his crotch, " 'Mr. Wiggly! We got us a job to do with these here magazines!' "

"Mr. Wiggily?" I ask, laughing.

"No. Not Wig-gi-ly. Wiggly. Wiggly," he corrects.

"Noted," I say, still laughing.

Then I hear my grandmother's voice. "Daniel!"

"Busted," Tim says as he guzzles his beer. I hand him the rest of my beer, and Tim guzzles the rest of that, too.

"Coming!" I call.

Tim puts the empty beer cans in his saddlebags. "Better let

you get back to work. Hey, come on down to the Elks lodge tonight."

"The Elks?" I say in disbelief. "You always swore you wouldn't."

"Yup. I'm an Elkoholic now. Raising money for children's charities while getting drunk. Bring that hot teacher if you can," he says.

Ha! As if I would do that to my worst enemy. "I'll get right on that," I say.

"My dad thinks I'm fixing fences, so kindly don't let it slip I was over here. I snuck through that gate you and me put in when we was fourteen. I still keep a bottle of Jack stashed under a pile of rocks there if you ever need it."

"Thanks, man."

Then he mounts up and rides off.

❧

My secret place is at the top of the hay bales next to the window that looks out on the barnyard. There's a loose board in the wall there that I move and pull out an old metal lunch box. I open it and inspect its contents: three small toy tractors and a dump truck, my mom's locket with a baby picture of me inside, and a picture of my parents when they were teenagers. I flip the picture over and look at the date written on the back, 1978. I flip it back over and look at it even closer. I bet it never occurred to them the day that picture was taken that they would die young. No teenager ever thinks they're actually going to die young. Then there's a program from their funeral. I look at it very briefly, wince, and put everything back in the lunch pail. I shut the lid and take a deep breath. Then I change my mind, open the pail again, take out the photo and the locket, slip them into my shirt pocket, shut the lunch pail, and slide it back behind the loose board in the barn wall.

From the window I can see Mara open the outdoor brick oven, shovel out some coals, and sweep the remaining ashes out. Grandma walks out of the house with some large balls of dough on a cookie sheet. Mara throws flour or something into the oven while Grandma places a ball of dough on a large wooden paddle. Mara picks up the paddle, places it in the oven, and jerks it so the dough slips off. I can hear their laughter and voices, but not what they're saying.

Mara pulls the cork from a bottle of red wine, pours two glasses, and lifts one to toast. Grandma lifts the other.

"To bread!" Mara shouts.

"To bread!" Grandma echoes. Huh? Grandma doesn't drink.

MARA

I've been working on creating the perfect sourdough starter. I've been moving it around to different places on the ranch to attract a wide spectrum of molds.

The fire is going quite nicely in the brick structure outside. When I'm sure it's hot enough, I'll put out the fire, then mop out the cinders and pop the dough in. I drool just thinking of the perfect crust.

Edith has joined me for the christening of the oven. Instead of breaking a bottle of wine over it, though, we are drinking it. She and I sip our Italian table wine while we push sun-dried to-mato chunks and garlic cloves into the bread. Is there anything better than focaccia bread? Not unless it's focaccia bread with baked elephant garlic and extra-virgin olive oil all over it.

"You know, Edith, I used to hate the word *lady*."

"Whatever for?"

"Sit like a lady, act like a lady, talk like a lady. The word seemed like a club to beat women back into submission."

She just laughs at me.

"But then my friend was teaching me to make bread dough and informed me that *lady* originally meant *she who kneads the bread*. She laughed and laughed at having turned me into a lady."

Edith laughs even more.

I refill our wineglasses before we take our beautiful loaves over to the oven.

Harvey watches us from his pen, sniffing the air and greeting us with little grunting noises that warm my heart.

Edith sits on the picnic table, leaning back with her feet up, while I mop out the cinders. "When the moon hits your eye like a big pizza pie, that's amore," she begins to sing, and I join her. Something about that song compels a person to hold up her wineglass while singing. At times we can't remember the words and sing, "Da, da, da . . ."

The singing attracts Earl who comes over to see what he's missing. I put the bread in and place a wooden door over the opening. He seems amused to find his wife tipsy. He leans over and whispers something in her ear, something I assume is sexy judging by Edith's flirtatious smile.

"I'm going to go now, dear!" she says to me. "Thank you! I had fun!" She drapes her arm around Earl and begins to stroll back to the house. I hear her sing on, "When you walk through a dream but you know you're not dreaming . . ."

❦

I know what my favorite thing on Earth is now. It's Zeus's fur. I love it. I love to bury my face in that really thick fur around his neck. You know, most people think dogs stink, but I find the smell rather comforting. Furry dogs are definitely my favorite thing on Earth. Better than warm wind. Better than fresh-baked bread. Even just a little better than the smell of horses or how their shoulder feels under your hand when you give them firm pats and that sound it makes. I do love it when a horse and I take turns breathing up each other's noses—I wonder what I must smell like to them—and their sweet peach-fuzzy nose is in my face. You gotta love those whiskery horse lips. And don't get me wrong: I'm developing quite a soft spot for hogs, too, but that thick fur around Zeus's neck and how safe I feel when I nuzzle my face in it, that takes the cake. I love Zeus.

I wonder how it all works, you know, with dogs and Heaven. Once, I overheard Tyler and the other fourth graders at his table discussing whether or not dogs went to regular people Heaven or if they have a special Dog Heaven.

I have a friend who suggested to me once that pets are souls you were really kind to in a past life who volunteer to come down in this form during this lifetime to be guardians. I don't know if I believe that or not, but I entertain the idea. I look at Zeus and wonder who he really is. I wonder what I did to deserve such a good dog friend.

You know, if dogs really are guardian souls, doesn't it make you sad to think of all those people keeping their dogs tied up in their backyards? Imagine treating a celestial being like a prisoner. Imagine not fully accepting your guardian. Do you suppose the guardian souls knew they'd end up chained in the same place for fifteen years when they volunteered to come down? Hard to imagine that. You know, there just aren't a lot of humans out there accepting all God's love in all its forms, if you ask me.

But maybe dogs are just dogs. And maybe they go to Dog Heaven. Or maybe they wait for us in one big Heaven. I hope so. I'd love to have this dog friend in Heaven, too. I'd bury my face in his neck for eternity.

Tonight, Zeus and I travel in our lucid dream to visit Gram

so I can show him off. He and I fly over the Gorge, Mount Adams, and Rainier, and land in Gram's front yard, in her angel garden among her numerous statues. Gram's spirit comes outside to greet us.

"Well, who do you have here?" she exclaims, reaching down to rub Zeus's belly.

"I wanted to show you my new dog!" I happily announce. "Hey, while you're up here, would you like to travel ahead a couple months and look at the tulip fields?" This is one of Gram's favorite things to do. Next thing I know, Gram, Zeus, and I are floating high in the sky above Mount Vernon's tulip fields in April. We wave to some people in a hot-air balloon, but they don't see us. Zeus smiles at birds passing us.

"I love this, don't you?" she asks me, a big smile on her face.

EARL

I'm bringin' in the yearlings for probably my last time. This is probably my last roundup, and not a very fast one, but that's all right because I want to savor it. I find myself wantin' to remember every detail about every past year's roundup. Heck, I find myself wantin' to remember every detail about my life. My brain won't do it, though. All the years blur together to make just one picture of my life.

There's somethin' about knowin' you're probably gonna die that makes you cowboy up and honestly live your last days. I'm aware of everything today. The air smells like horse and cattle and that smell of fall. I can't believe this is probably the last fall I'm gonna smell.

I now realize how many years I wasted feeling dead after the kids died. I just sorta functioned without much thinking for the last twenty-four years. I'm not sayin' that I shouldn't've grieved. I'm just sayin' that at some point I should've woke up. I guess at some point grief became a habit, and then it became who I was. Guess there's no use cryin' over spilt milk.

But I do look at Daniel and see the same thing—just sorta functioning. And I wonder if he would be this way if I had been there for him. I thought I was there for him. I never missed a rodeo. Maybe he needed something else from me. I don't know. All I know is I would hate for him, like me, to have to be facing his death before he learns to enjoy his life.

Mara, Whitey, and I pull up the rear, followed, of course, by Zeus and that damned hog, Harvey. Daniel and Hank ride the sides. When we get the herd into a draw that deepens as we continue gradually downhill, Daniel and Hank are able to kick back with us a little more.

Hank rides over to Mara. "You know, my daughter is in your class."

"Oh, yeah? Who's that?" Mara asks.

"Allison O'Callighan," he answers.

"Neat kid. Good job," she says.

"Did she tell you what I did to her at the fair?" Hank asks.

"No," she says.

"Well, I'm the rodeo announcer there, and I look over and spot my daughter by the hog barn talkin' to some boys, so I say over the intercom, 'Hey, you boys by the hog barn talkin' to my daughter! I'm the big guy up here in the red shirt, and I'm Allison's dad! I just bought a new twenty-two, and I'm a good shot!'"

"Oh, I bet she was horrified. Has she forgiven you yet?"

"Well, I think she almost did, but I speculate I may have made things worse when I passed by her at the football game last week and saw some kid holdin' her hand. I went, 'Hey! You holdin' my daughter's hand?' Well the kid jerked his hand away like this and says, 'No, sir!' and so I said, 'Good, 'cause if you were, I was gonna have to rip off your hand and beat you with it.' "

"Allison is one lucky girl," Mara says.

Then, just for fun, I shout out, "Hey, Mara, mouse!"

"Very funny," she says.

"Hank, Daniel. Okay now, this is better than the fact that she has a pet hog. I'm looking out my window yesterday and see Mara get in her foreign pickup," I begin.

"Don't start, Earl. You know Toyotas are manufactured in Detroit now," she interrupts.

"She's about to drive off," I continue, "when she jumps out and does this wild dance." I imitate her a little, but it spooks the horse. "She looks in her pickup from time to time, still runnin', and she's all shuddering like this. So eventually I go out to see what the fuss is about. She sees me and starts shrieking, 'There was a mouse on my shoulder!' "

"I didn't sound anything like that, Earl. You're exaggerating."

"God as my witness, I swear I am not. 'Now, Earl, I've never had a problem with mice, but it was so close to my neck, Earl! My neck!' and she starts with that eebie-jeebie dance again. Now, she wasn't about to get back in that truck again even though I told her I was quite sure the little bugger had jumped out through the firewall about the time she slammed on the brakes. She was havin' none of it."

"So what did you do?" Whitey asks.

"What do you think I did? I reached in, turned off the damn engine, grabbed the nearest barn cat, threw it in, and shut the door!"

"Shoot," says Whitey and starts laughing. Whitey is even older than me and likes to tell stories of ridin' the pack trains up the Icicle Canyon above Leavenworth, Washington, as a kid. He was quite a bull rider in his day, too. "I remember once a mouse was livin' in the heatin' system of my truck. Then he died. Sure made an awful stink. Then a few months later when winter came, I turned on my heater, and all these dried mouse parts come shootin' out of the vent!" He laughs sort of raspy like old men do.

Then Hank chimes in: "Once, I got into a pickup I had parked in a field for maybe two weeks. I put my foot down on the clutch and felt a squish and sorta heard a crunch. Well, I tell you what, I look down at the bottom of my boot, and there's squished baby mice all over it!"

"Did you track 'em all over your wife's carpet?" Whitey is really heehawing.

"Nope. Just took the nearest stick and scraped 'em out." Hank's laugh is so deep and low, I swear only elephants can hear it. "Hey, is anyone else's butt getting sore, or is it just me?"

Everyone agrees.

Hank says, "I never did understand people who rode for pleasure. Ridin' was somethin' we had to do, and during most of the year we were hatin' every minute of it."

"Cold," Whitey says.

I agree. "Yeah, miserable, cold rain."

Hank says, "This is the year I'm gonna trade in my horses for four-wheelers. Hey, Mara, want to buy a horse, or are you going to eventually break that hog? I figure if you're not going to eat it, you should at least figure out a way to ride it."

"I'll get right on that," she says.

"You could ride it in parades," Hank says with a laugh.

"Hey, Mara," Daniel says. "If Hank starts giving you too bad of a time about your hog, you just ask him how Fifi is."

Whitey and I begin to laugh hysterically.

"Fifi, huh?" Mara asks, delighted.

"Yeah, Hank, why isn't Fifi riding with you today?" Whitey asks, tears streaming down his face with laughter.

"Let me tell you a little story about Hank," I begin.

"Don't believe a word they say, Mara," Hank says.

"Now Hank had this pitbull that used to follow him when he rode his motorcycle into town—" I start.

"I loved that dog. Buddy," Hank says.

I continue, "—but one time Mrs. Gallagher's shih tzu ran out at them. The pitbull killed it and brought it to Hank, so there was no denying how the shih tzu died. Well, Mrs. Gallagher claimed it was a five-hundred-dollar dog, and Hank wasn't about to fork that over, so he found her a three-hundred-dollar shih tzu and brought it to her."

Hanks says, "She kept it for a few days but didn't like it, so she called me and asked me to take it away. The breeder I got it from wouldn't take it back, so I was stuck with this three-hundred-dollar yap-yap."

"Though he publicly curses the dog, it should be noted you never see Hank driving around on his motorcycle without it," I say. Mara laughs.

"It just sits right there on the gas tank and yaps at everything it passes," Whitey says.

"He put those no-slip stickers for shower floors right on the gas tank for the dog, so it won't slip off," I say.

"Damn little rat dog," Hank says.

I catch Daniel shooting pictures of all of us telling stories, and I'm glad. I want to be remembered like this.

It's probably my last roundup and my last autumn. I hope Heaven is so wonderful that I won't miss this life, but that's hard for me to imagine. Just when I find myself gettin' lost in these thoughts, Hank starts up with another story. I give my horse a couple firm pats on the shoulder and drink up this day like a fine shot of brandy.

DANIEL

"If you have to go on the crab boat for just three weeks, why don't you just fly there and then fly back when it's over? That way you can spend Christmas with us. Daniel, it's been so long, and life is short," Grandma says.

She played the card. I can't believe Grandma played the card. Now what can you do when your grandma plays the "I'm not going to be here forever" card? You can't dismiss it. You can't blow her off. She would think she didn't matter to you. I pause a moment and study her. Yep, she is not going to live forever. I see a fragility I never used to see in her eyes. I can't say no. I can't say no to her. "Okay," I say.

I just signed myself up for November, December, and January on the ranch. Three months. Three long and quiet winter months. Shit.

❦

The drive to the Portland airport is a beautiful one. The road winds next to the steep basalt cliffs and wide, choppy river. Autumn has turned the shrub oak high on the cliffs as well as the apple trees and vine maples down in the valley. A few hearty windsurfers still tear through the Gorge, clinging to brightly colored sails.

I try to imagine early settlers running this river on log rafts back in the days before the dams, back when the river flowed with all its force. It's incredible that any of them made it through alive. It must have been quite a river when it was wild and free. The dams seem permanent to me, but I know that in the larger picture few things are forever. One day the dams will crumble, and people may or may not still be here to rebuild them. Tough to say. I wonder whether the only way to freedom is through devastation. This country had to have a devastating war with England to be free. All over the world there are examples of that. Natural disasters are devastating. Do they ever lead to freedom? I guess if having your trailer picked up and spun around in the air is your idea of free, then, yes, it leads to freedom. But most of the time I think it could be argued that natural disasters don't lead to freedom—for people at least.

If I were that river, my dams would have been built when I lost my parents. Would more devastation blow those away, or would more devastation just lead to the construction of more dams?

I find a parking lot that charges twelve bucks a day. That's going to add up. The shuttle bus takes me to the airport where I kill time by walking and noticing the differences in people who are going to different locations. People going to Seattle and Anchorage wear a lot of polar fleece and hiking boots. You see a lot of backpacks in that crowd. People going to Kansas City look soft and bored, but kind. The Pittsburgh crowd looks hardened and edgy. I think the least attractive people are headed for Albuquerque, although the Cleveland crowd leaves a little to be desired, too. Dallas and New York groups are by far the loudest. The difference is that the Dallas people exchange friendly loud stories with one another while the New York crowd shouts into cell phones. The women going to Dallas have hair that doesn't move. I return to gate B10 and sit with the polar fleece and backpack people.

❧

The pot launcher drops a string of thirty crab pots into the ocean. The captain tells us how and when to lay them and how quickly to bring them up. Sometimes we leave them down for ten to twelve hours. Other times we bring them up in forty-five minutes. Altogether we have about two hundred pots, each one about six by six by two feet.

We are all back in our rhythm, the orchestration of many unspoken tasks.

I pick crabs up by their backs and think to myself, You live, you live, you die. You die, you die, and you die. You live for now, but we'll get you next year.

I wonder if this is what it feels like to be God. If so, it doesn't feel all that great. I feel a little more like the Grim Reaper. The Grim Reaper doesn't make judgments like God; he just carries out the orders. When your time's up, your time's up, simple as that. And since there's not a lot of crabs down there singing their babies to sleep or reading them bedtime stories, I don't feel too bad about it.

EDITH

I knock on Mara's door just before supper. "I just heard we're supposed to get our first frost tonight. Time to harvest everything. Want to help?" The sun is already setting, and I need all the help I can get before it gets dark.

"You bet," she says. She steps out and breathes in deeply. "I love this. You can feel the change coming."

"Crisp," I say as we walk toward the garden. First we pluck all the tomatoes off the vines. "There's something very nice about having green tomatoes on my windowsills this time of year. You know last year some didn't ripen until around Christmas. Homegrown tomatoes on Christmas. Can you imagine?"

"That right there is the good life," she says. "Homegrown tomatoes. You can't buy that kind of happiness."

"No, indeed," I agree. I admire the lush vines that will be

dead tomorrow, and marvel at how their fruits will nourish me long after they're gone. I hope I will be like that when it's my time. I hope I'll leave behind something akin to green tomatoes on people's windowsills that will nourish them long after I'm gone. And then my moment of acceptance toward my own mortality turns uncomfortable, so I leave the rest of the tomatoes for Mara to pick and begin to pull carrots instead.

She picks green beans. A chilly gust blows golden leaves from the apple and pear trees, not yet crunchy, toward us. "Leaves!" she exclaims. "God, I love autumn leaves!"

"Help yourself to whatever of this you think you can eat," I say as I pick several squashes. I like squash, but I don't like it quite this much.

"Thanks! Maybe I'll make a stew!" she says.

"Spinach should be okay. Potatoes we want to freeze. Pick that lettuce, though. That will be the first to go."

"I feel like a squirrel collecting acorns for the winter," she jokes. "I just love October."

I pick up an especially beautiful gold leaf. "Wouldn't it be great if a person whose hair was turning white or gray was looked upon as just as beautiful as an autumn tree?" I say. I pull a knife out of my pocket and begin to cut broccoli.

"I love gray hair," she says. "I can't understand why anyone would color it."

That's easy to say when you're still in the July of your life. When I first reached October, I was alarmed to find my hair reminding me that December was right around the corner.

We put all the vegetables in plastic shopping bags. "Let's go wash this in my kitchen," I say. We walk side by side back to the house under the twilight sky, our hands filled with bags and bags of mostly tomatoes. It's a good feeling.

And as we wash the produce and fill my windowsills, I am

grateful to have her presence in the house. I've been feeling Daniel's absence this week, to put it mildly. It's so hard to finally get him back, only to have to let him go again, even though I know it's just for two more weeks. When those feelings come up, I just think about Christmas, like how I'll hang three stockings by the fireplace this year, things like that.

I glance up and am delighted to see a blazing orange harvest moon rise over the horizon. "Mara, look!" I say. "I'm in love with the man on the moon," I start to sing. To my surprise she joins in.

"I love that song," she says when it's over. "Gram used to sing that to me all the time."

The wind blows Earl into the house along with a few leaves. "Mara. Good to see you in the kitchen," he says as he takes off his boots.

"Don't start with me, Earl," she says with a smile.

Then to my surprise Earl walks over and gives me a kiss on the cheek. I catch a mischievous glimmer in his eye, and it makes me feel like an apple tree crowned with radiant autumn leaves—just beginning to realize my full glory.

EARL

There are three places a man can get his wife flowers: the Red Apple grocery store, Murray's Drug Store, and in a field somewhere. In October a man only has two of those choices, and both places come with an audience. Now I have learned from Hank on his anniversary that a man cannot get out of Murray's with a dozen roses for less than twenty-five bucks. Red Apple has more reasonable prices but a less reliable selection.

I examine my choices there at the end of the produce aisle—pink or yellow. Now it's the pink ones that remind me of when

I first met Edith. I like pink a lot. Not for me, of course, but for her. I mean, can you picture me in a pink shirt, or better yet a pink suit? Oh, man, the boys would pay money to see that. But I like pink roses for Edith. I think of how when I whisper something suggestive in her ear, her cheeks light up that color. Truth be told, I think the pink and the yellow are prettier than red. Red isn't as bright, not as happy. Still, I know red says love. Red says romance. Edith probably wants to receive red. But I really like the pink ones. Damn, I wish someone wrote a manual for situations like these. You'd think after nearly sixty years, I'd have it figured out. I have no clue.

"In the dog house, Earl?" I hear Whitey's voice. Damn. If Daniel were with me on this errand, I could have made it look like he was getting them for somebody. Well, I guess I knew I'd never get out of here without a witness. I just chuckle and avoid his question. "Say something stupid?"

I guess a man who's been married as long as me can't get his lovely wife some flowers just because he appreciates her? "Oh, you know me," I say, again dodging this conversation as best I can. "What do you think?" I ask. "I like these here pink ones."

"Yeah, those are nice," Whitey says.

"The yellow ones are nice, too," I say.

"Irene once told me that women think yellow roses are for friendship," he says.

"No yellow then," I say. "What about pink?"

"Hey, Sandy," Whitey says to Sandy as she passes. Sandy works at the bank. I'm guessing she's in her midforties. She wears too much makeup. "What do pink roses say to a woman?"

"You getting roses for someone, Whitey? You sly old dog! Who? I swear I won't tell a soul," she says. Oh, damn. I can see this one coming. The whole damn town is going to know my business by noon on Monday.

"Oh, not me. Earl here is picking some out for his wife," Whitey says.

"Earl, what'd you do?" she asks accusingly.

"You guys are awful quick to assume the worst about me. I'm hurt. I really am," I say, trying to joke my way out of any real conversation about my motives. I am not about to tell either one of them about what went on in my bedroom last night.

"Uh-huh," Sandy says suspiciously. "Well, pink is for innocent love. When a boy brings my daughter pink or yellow flowers, I think it's cute. But the boy who brings my daughter red roses is the boy who is going to get castrated by my husband."

We chuckle. "Thank you, Sandy. You've been a great help," I say, and after she goes on her way, I say, "And thank you, Whitey, for now the whole damn town is going to be speculating on the state of my marriage."

Whitey laughs me off. "Oh, Earl, the whole damn town would be speculating on the state of your marital affairs the minute you got in the checkout line anyway."

"Yeah, you're right," I consent. "Well, I'm off to plan B," I say.

"Good luck, Earl. Flowers are a good move. Next time she asks you something, remember not to hesitate before you answer. Never, never hesitate."

I give him a wave as I walk out of the Red Apple and across the street to Murray's. I wander back to the flower counter and look in the refrigerator. Barb Murray puts down the bandages she's restocking and comes back to help me.

"Why, hello, Earl. What can I do for you today?" she asks.

"I would like a dozen red roses, please," I say uncomfortably.

"Is it a special anniversary?" she asks.

"Something like that," I say.

And then from behind me I hear the unmistakable booming voice of Hank. "Oh, Earl, tell the truth. You made your wife mad, didn't you?" The whole damn town can hear him whenever he opens his mouth. This is not happening. "A dozen? Boy, you must have really messed up bad. Do I dare ask what exactly you said?" I can just hear the rumors now. I hope none of them get back to Edith. These roses could actually do more harm than good.

As I think about my reply, I notice the prescription bag in Hank's hand. "That funny rash of yours clear up yet, Hank?" I ask. When it comes to the rumor mill, the best defense is a great offense.

"What are you talking about?" he asks. "These are my blood pressure pills," he says.

"Oh, sorry," I say. "I should have known that given the location of your rash, it was hush-hush."

He takes the bottle out of the bag. "Take one twice daily with meals to lower blood pressure," he reads.

"That will be twenty-five dollars," Barb says.

I slap down my cash, get my flowers, and prepare to high-tail it out of there before the subject can be turned back to me. "Well, good luck with that," I say to Hank and make my rapid exit.

But all of it is worth it when I walk through the door and see Edith's face light up. "Oh, Earl," she says and puts her arms around me. "Oh, Earl, they're beautiful." Then she plants quite a kiss on me. As I kiss her back, I spin her into a little dip. "Oh, Earl," she says with a giggle. And I suddenly remember how much we used to laugh, before Sam was born, before the accident, and all the crazy antics I did to get that giggle out of her. I would have done anything for that giggle back then, and hearing it again now, I feel the same. I look at her soft face and into her big blue eyes, and I think there is nothing I wouldn't do for this woman. Nothing.

EDITH

Mara and I are bundled up, and our saddlebags are full of the applesauce we spent all day making. The sun is down now, and the moon is full. We are going on a secret mission to give away applesauce and apples to three single mothers Mara knows can use it. We agreed we want them to have this food anonymously so they won't have to say thank-you, because they shouldn't have to say thank-you. So we're riding several miles into town on horseback by cutting through Owen's pasture. We're going on an adventure.

Zeus puts his paws on the windowsill of the Church of the Dog and stares out at us. He's not happy about being left behind.

Harvey paces back and forth, excited, and Mara speculates that every time he's seen her on a horse, it meant he was going to get to tag along for the day, so he probably expects this time will be no different. We both agree, though, that it wouldn't really be practical to have a hog following us through town.

Earl asked me to check fences while we're out there. I laughed at him.

We mount up to begin our journey and start out the back pasture. We have to go in the wrong direction for a little bit until we find the gate to Owen's place. After we cross, we try staying on the hilltops, above where deep draws have carved their paths into hillsides. The wind blows crisp autumn smells to us as we ride down the hills that will take us to town.

"You know, Edith, I realize I'm wearing clothes and that

I'm dealing with the aftereffects of fertility rather than blessing others with fertility, but I still sort of feel like Lady Godiva!" she shouts as we trot away.

"Well, I suppose we are all secretly riding at night and trying to make things better!" I shout back and make that face I make when I shrug.

She bellows a wild call, and the horses get jumpy with excitement. How exactly we are going to be inconspicuous in town on horseback at 1:00 a.m. I don't know, but the risk of it all gives me a sense of adventure that makes me feel like a girl again.

As we approach town and slow down, Mara talks about wanting to grow a garden next year especially for the purpose of harvesting and distributing on our Lady Godiva runs. I suggest we have a Lady Godiva run this winter before the snows get too deep and distribute fresh-baked bread, noting that the snow will muffle the horses' hooves.

The only person who spots us is Dawson, an officer and old friend, in his patrol car. We just smile, wave, and ride on.

On the way home, though, Mara says, "I don't know if I'll ever be pregnant, but if I ever am, I want a really gentle horse so that I can still ride, and even ride with the baby, too."

I cringe. "I lost a baby because I was riding when I was pregnant," I say.

"Oh," she says. "I'm sorry."

"It was on a safe horse. Just one of those freak accidents. I tell women now that nine months is such a short time compared to a lifetime of guilt."

There is an awkward silence, but it's worth it. It's worth it if I made my point, if I can spare another woman my experience.

I remember riding Molasses, just poking along next to a fence line. The balsam flowers were blooming mini sunflowers.

The flowers were yellow, the sky was blue, my horse was yellow, my jeans and shirt were blue. This is what I was thinking about before Molasses saw that snake and jumped back. He took three steps back and hit the fence line, which really spooked him. He leaped forward, remembered the snake, and twisted midair so he would land somewhere else. And I remember that split second of flying.

I remember the pain in my abdomen as I opened my eyes, and when my thoughts turned to my worst fears, I began to cry. Molasses hovered over me as I attempted to get to my feet. He sniffed me to see if I was okay, his eyes saying how sorry he was. I buckled over again. Then I grabbed a stirrup and crawled up the saddle to my feet. Molasses held perfectly still as I got into the saddle, crying out with each sharp pain. I don't know how I made it into the saddle except that thought is powerful, and I thought that maybe if I could get to the hospital, my baby, our baby, would be okay. But it wasn't.

I spent two weeks in the hospital hemorrhaging and recovering. Earl, concerned, sat by my side, but there was something else in his eyes, too—"If only . . . if only . . . if only"—feeding my guilt and shame and my own long list of if onlys.

I knew I'd never put myself before my child again, but it was too late for this one, and, as it turned out, for any others besides Sam. The child I lost was a little girl. I so wanted a little girl. My precious little girl would live on only as a pain in my heart. Nine months is such a short time, such a short time.

❧

It's interesting how someone who is making choices so different from mine can respect and appreciate my choices so much. They weren't choices, really. They were merely what was expected of me. Nonetheless, she points out the strength with which I led my life—the strength I failed to recognize.

She appears on the surface to be so strong, but in my heart I know I'm stronger. I think she is afraid to love. With me it's not a choice. I endured the most painful thing anyone can, the loss of two children, and somehow I kept my will to continue to love. Even now as I approach the end of my life, facing the fact that Earl and I probably won't be able to synchronize our exits and that I may be left to spend my last years without the very one I poured all my heart into, even now, I am not afraid to love.

I think Mara would be content to live in that tiny Church of the Dog until her heart atrophies to the size of her small, one-woman home.

Interesting how women could make such supposedly great strides in knowing and asserting their worth, but in ways that are quite basic they've lost it all together. They don't even understand what it means to be a woman.

MARA

I open the door to let Zeus out and see snowflakes falling. Oh, dear. I hope I don't get misunderstood and burned at the stake for this.

See, I had the kindergartners today and no lesson plans. So I got them cutting snowflakes while I assembled a custom-fit, three-foot-tall cone hat for each child out of blue butcher paper. I told them we were making magic snow hats and that if they wished for snow while wearing the hats, it would snow before Christmas—unless they lose the power in their snow hat. Being mean or whining while wearing the magic snow hat will cause it to lose its power, I told them. I sent them off at the end of class in their paper hats, in most cases taller than the child wearing it, and didn't think much more about it until now.

I step out and lift my head so that the snowflakes land on my cheeks like kisses from the Universe. This is the way to go. The Universe is capable of so much more love than another person.

Still, I wonder what my friend from the Grand Canyon is doing now. Maybe the Universe is kissing him, too. I send my own good energy up into the Universe to be part of that just in case.

Then my moment is over as I regain awareness of the two hundred calves crying out for their mothers as they adjust to being weaned. I wish I could get away from here until the weaning is over. Most of the calves will be sent off to become meat. I wonder if on some level they know. I imagine them like Disney characters calling out for their mommy like Bambi did: "Mommy! Mommy! Don't let them take me away and kill me!" Try to fall asleep listening to that.

While Edith milks her nurse cows, I start a fire in the little tin stove and take the bucket to a faucet on the side of Edith and Earl's house. Saunas are now part of my Saturday morning ritual with Edith. Since the sun takes longer to rise, Earl spends more time at the café.

The second after Earl leaves for town, Edith and I streak out to the sauna in nothing but our towels.

Mostly we talk about what it means to be a woman and where our true strengths lie. I love to listen to her talk about her life, her views, her hindsight, her acceptance, her love.

I've based my self-value as a woman on my potential, my opportunity, whereas she sees her value as a woman as intrinsic. This is a very important lesson for me.

On this morning Edith looks at me with a sparkle in her eye. "Let's go make snow angels!" she says. My only reply is a delighted smile.

We run out of the sauna, dive into the powdery snow, and make snow angels. We are laughing so hard that we're crying. We do this about six more times before Edith goes back to her house to receive this week's roses from Earl, who has become quite a romantic devil in recent weeks. I go back to the Church of the Dog to prepare to fix fences and shrink Earl's tumor.

I've discovered I can actually shrink it better when my hands are on him, so I continue to invite myself over on Friday nights for short dance lessons. I've got the fox-trot down now, my waltz is improving, and I'm getting into the cha-cha.

Now that Earl and I have to bundle up a little more to check fences, these are my only times to get a good look at the bump. Lately it seems like it's growing more during the week than I can shrink it.

EARL

Mara helps me sort this year's calves. I pick out the best-quality heifers, the ones with the greatest length and width, the best bags with the smallest tits, and the ones with feminine-looking heads. They'll stay in my small feed lot so I can give them good feed this winter.

The ones who won't be staying get even better feed—corn and barley silage supplemented with vitamins, minerals, and protein. The nutritionist says it should help them gain two and a half to three pounds a day.

In the next few weeks we'll separate the big steers, too. The big ones will be sent away in mid-December, while the small steers will be fed for another month along with the feeder heifers and sent away in January.

When I explain what we are doing to Mara, she seems a little distressed at the fact that she's become, in her own words, "the angel of death at Cattle Auschwitz." I wish Daniel would have stayed and helped with this. Maybe I need to get Whitey out here.

"Earl, last night I noticed you have two bumps on your neck now," Mara says as we unsaddle the horses and put the tack away.

"Thanks for noticing," I say. I can tell by her eyes that she knows. I think she's known for a long time. We walk to the barn and back, and then brush out the horses. "Red, I don't reckon I'll be around much longer."

She looks concerned.

"Will you watch over Edith when I'm gone?"

"Absolutely."

"When it melts off in the spring, get Daniel to help you with the fences. The deer and elk will have knocked a lot of them down, so you'll have to check them all again."

"I will."

I know she will keep her word.

"Maybe you can make me a list of repairs you can think of that I might otherwise not know to do."

We walk the horses back to their paddock and turn them loose. My eyes get blurry as I think about leaving behind my beloved Edith. Mara is respectful enough not to look. I wonder if I've deserved Edith all these years.

Mara stops and gives her hog a bucket of pig feed and a couple Oreos.

"Red, what do you think happens to folks when they die?"

"I've heard some people say that when you first cross over, you get to experience your life with panoramic vision and feel all the things you made others feel," Mara says. "Yeah. I don't pretend to know what happens, but I believe it's good. My Gram says she's not going to die. She says she's going to 'ascend.' Says she's going to take her body with her. Uncle Bob told her to please leave a note when she goes so we don't spend a lot of time looking for her or anything. Other people in my family believe that you come to Earth to learn or experience something, and when your business is finished, you get to 'graduate.' Gram liked that idea for a while and even made me promise to wear a Happy Graduation hat to her service when she goes, but these days I think she's viewing the graduation idea as a little too judgmental. I don't know if I completely agree with the graduation idea, either, because it implies Earth life is about work. Maybe it's not. Maybe it's like a vacation from all our work in Heaven, only we are born with no memory of Heaven so we don't ruin our vacation by thinking about work. Hm . . . I don't know, Earl. Maybe Heaven is whatever you want it to be."

"I've always hoped it would be a big family reunion. And I've always hoped there would be a café up there so that when I got sick of all that family, all those aunts and grandmas yakkin' on and such, I could go to that café and tell stories with all my old dead friends." I pause. "Think everyone gets there?"

"Yup," she replies.

"Yup, me, too," I say. "Even all those sickos. Just makes sense to me that after they leave their sick mind in a hole in the earth, they would go Home."

Mara nods. "Is that why you never join Edith going to church? Because it doesn't really match your common sense?"

"Yup, that, and this is my church." I gesture at the land and the sky with my hand. "All this. Always thought God was probably too big to fit in a tiny little crowded building where all the seats are already taken. I might go again soon just to make Edith happy, though. What about you, Red? How come you never go to church?"

"I don't believe those ministers know anything we don't. I

figure, why deal with a middleman when you can buy wholesale, you know? Ministers remind me of used car salesmen. I believe religion is what happens when ego contaminates spirituality. I believe the truth is in our hearts. God lives in our hearts. God speaks to us in our hearts if we shut up long enough to listen." Pause. Then she adds self-consciously, "I believe, anyway."

"Amen," I say solemnly. She turns on the water for the horses while I check the water for the calves. I watch the hog and the dog sniff this or that together and then run off side by side to sniff something else.

"Are you scared, Earl?"

"Yeah. Yes and no. Mostly I'm scared that my wife and grandson will never know what they meant to me." I pause and look her in the eye for a minute.

She nods. "You know, Earl, I see your silhouettes in the window after I leave my dancing lessons. I think you've made your time count . . . since I've known you, anyway. I know Edith feels deeply loved by you."

I nod. I hope so. She's probably right. Shame to leave Edith just when the sparks are startin' to fly again.

MARA

In my dream I'm standing in a big feed lot with my Angel who brought me here. Numbers are called out on a loudspeaker outside the slaughterhouse, and when they are, corresponding cattle willfully run into the slaughterhouse. Number seventy-eight runs right in front of me with her head up. She is proud. And I get it: To feed others is honorable. She is proud of her sacrifice. I feel a little better about the whole beef situation, and the dream ends.

Daniel returned yesterday. Earl sent us out to gather strays today.

"I feel guilty sitting on this old man," I say with regard to the ancient palomino I was told to ride today. "Are you sure I'm not hurting him?"

"I'm not sure," Daniel answers. "He might have arthritis or just aches and pains. I don't know. But look at him. His head is high, and he looks happy. Pal was quite a cutting horse in his day, and you know, I think he knew he was the best. I think he was proud of that. I think it's been really hard on him to be left behind while younger horses went off to do the work he used to enjoy doing."

"Everyone likes to be important, I suppose," I say.

"Everyone needs to have a purpose," he says. "How many times have you heard of someone dropping dead right after they retire? All the time. Animals need jobs, too. Border collies chewing up everything in city apartments need to have a job. They get bored and depressed without a job. Grandpa had you ride Pal today because he knew Pal was getting depressed. Now Pal may be a little uncomfortable, but he's not depressed anymore. Who's to say whether arthritis hurts worse than boredom and depression?"

"Good point," I say.

"There they are," he says. "We're going to ride wide around them. You go that way, and I'll go this way. This should be easy."

That was the end of our conversation.

I felt a little better about bringing in cattle to be slaughtered after my dream, but it's still hard for me. I think a little meat is probably good for most people. A little. I look at the young steer closest to me. There is honor in feeding others who need to be fed. Is there honor in being an excessively large steak for a morbidly obese person? I don't know. Something about it seems sad to me. Wasteful. I imagine someone being served a part of that steer and throwing away the rest of their steak, throwing away the whole reason he sacrificed his life. People think vegetarians see meat as a black-and-white thing, and maybe some do. I wish I could see it all as clearly as that, but I don't. For me it's not black and white. Ethical implications of my actions and choices are never simple or easy to me. At the same time I recognize it's a luxury to be able to take ethics into consideration. Most people in this world are just trying to survive. And I am no one to judge any of them.

DANIEL

I open my eyes to the sound of laughter coming from outside. Laughter in and around this house—imagine that. Grandma drinking wine, Grandpa buying roses and dancing in the living room. Sometimes I want to ask Mara what she did with my real grandparents.

I groan and sit up. My body still aches from riding all day yesterday looking for stray cattle that got left behind on the first roundup. I groan more and massage my legs.

I peek out the window to see what the laughter is about, and to my horror, see my grandmother and Mara naked, making snow angels in about five inches of new snow. Grandma gets up and runs back into the little sauna. I put my hand over my eyes. I think seeing that physically hurt me. I grimace and shudder. Now Grandma's running around naked. What's next?

I shake it off and look again. Mara lies still in the snow for a minute, leisurely stands, and looks around her as if she can feel me watching. She looks up, catches me, smiles, and waves. Then she walks casually back to the sauna.

I rub my forehead with my hand, embarrassed.

ᴇᴀʀʟ

There are three goddamned bumps on my neck today. The first one is huge and painful now.

I walk down the staircase, past the pictures of all the people in our family, now dead, and figure my picture will be up on that wall before too long.

When I get to the breakfast table, Edith is in the middle of askin' Daniel whether there's a special woman in his life.

"Nope," he says, and I'm not surprised bein' that he's always been a loner n'all. Edith looks sad about that, and I can tell she wants to ask him more questions, but Daniel doesn't look up from his eggs.

I walk over and kiss my wife on the cheek as she scrambles more eggs. She smiles at me and warms my heart. I catch Daniel looking puzzled. "What are you looking at?" I ask defensively. He shrugs.

Mara knocks on the door and lets herself in. "Good morning! Fencing today? The snow is melting fast."

"Nah. Yesterday was a long day. Come in," I say. We all rode about fourteen hours.

"Roses!" says Mara.

I change the subject abruptly. "Hey, want to see something funny? Daniel, will you please bring me that cup behind you?" Daniel picks up my cup of coffee and hobbles over to the table, expecting to see something funny. "Thanks," I say to him. Then I turn to Mara. "Daniel's a little sore today." I laugh. "Isn't that funny?"

Daniel goes back to buttering toast while Mara sits across from me at the table. She looks up at me and points to her neck. I attempt to cover up the bumps with my shirt. She holds up three fingers. Daniel turns around and sees that.

"Grandpa, is she telling you that on a scale of one to ten, she thinks I'm a three?" he asks, joking.

When I noticed my new bump this morning, I had resolved that today would be the day I told 'em. There is no good time to do it. Best just to do it. "There's no easy way to tell you this," I start, but chicken out. "Daniel, but yes."

Mara's concerned expression alerts Edith and Daniel that there is something serious going on.

"Well, actually, no. She was pointing out that there are three bumps on my neck today. There was only one a couple months ago. There's no good way or right time to say this, so I'm just going to say it: I think my days are numbered." There, I said it. They just stare at me.

"Well, maybe you should go to the doctor," Edith says angrily.

"Name one person we know who has gone in the hospital and then come out," I say.

Mara and Daniel look at their eggs.

"You're giving up just like that," Edith says.

They stare at me kind of blankly, and I get to feelin' a little uncomfortable. "If you'll excuse me, I'm going to go check to see if all the livestock water is froze up."

I go outside and take a few deep breaths before I begin to make my way to the trough.

DANIEL

Grandma and I just sort of look at each other for a few minutes. I suspect Grandpa's announcement feels more real to her than it does to me. I wish I could say something comforting to her, but instead I just sit there, knowing I should do something but do nothing.

"Well, what'd'ya think? He was going to live forever?" She seems angry and I'm not sure if she's talking to me or herself.

"Excuse me," I say quietly. I walk over to the door, pull on my boots, and grab my camera.

I walk out to where I find Grandpa with his arms folded over the top of the paddock fence. I rest my forearms there, too, and sort of drop my head through the empty space between my arms. Eventually, I lift my head up to look at Grandpa staring down at me with a gentleness I've not often seen on his face.

"Grandpa? Can I take a few pictures of you?" I respectfully ask.

"I don't know. You any good at it? I don't want people re-memberin' me as some ugly old guy. Can you make me look about forty years younger? Or at least make me look like that Clint Eastwood fella everyone thinks is the cat's meow."

I laugh a little and capture Grandpa peering out over his December steers and his land, the siding on the barn behind him as weathered as his face.

"So what are you gonna do with your inheritance, boy?"

"You know, Grandpa, I was thinking of selling all the cattle and buying some of those little miniature horses that pull carts at the fair." Joking around has been the way Grandpa and I avoid talking about anything real. This time I joke to dodge the question I'd rather not think about, and he seems relieved and laughs.

"Hey, remember when you were about fifteen and just takin' an interest in the bulls? You were on that big black Angus we bought from the McDaniels. Whitey and I were standin' right here talkin' about how it seemed you were a natural when that bull sent you flyin' right over our heads. Hoo!" He laughs so hard, he cries. "Oh, you were just like that Superman for all of three seconds!" He holds his sides now, laughing so hard.

We both retreat to our trenches, hiding safely behind our humor. "Jesus, Grandpa, weren't you scared I'd break my neck? I remember that fall. Knocked the wind out of me for about four days, cracked six ribs, and just about scared the life out of Grandma, who, as I recall, came running out of the house calling you every name in the book. It was the only time I ever heard words like that pass Grandma's lips. She had a few words for Whitey, too, if I remember right." Grandpa laughs hard, tracing my path in the sky with his finger. "How'd your marriage survive that, anyway?"

He laughs and pats me on the shoulder until his arm comes to rest on the other shoulder. "You know, boy, I'm not sure I ever told you just how proud I was, am, of you. Not for the bull riding. Just for turning out reasonably well." He gives me an extra squeeze on my shoulder and says, "You mean the world to me, boy."

I'm a little startled and for a moment feel a little naked. But then I put my arm around Grandpa.

"You know, Grandpa, I respect your choice to skip chemo if you really are dying, but I think for Grandma's sake you need to get a diagnosis. I mean, maybe they're just fatty cysts like Blue used to get."

"You're comparing me to a dog?"

"I'm just saying learn what all your options are so that your choice is the best one. And I think you need to listen to what Grandma wants even if you don't choose it. I think you owe her that," I say.

"Okay, Dr. Phil," he says.

❦

When Grandpa and I enter the clinic, I can see he's worried. I take a seat in the waiting area while he checks in with the receptionist. Then he returns and sits next to me on a light blue vinyl chair. We leaf neverously and silently through issues of *Sunset* and *Family Circle*. I'm not really even paying attention to what's on the pages. It just feels good to turn them.

Grandpa looks at me sideways. "You lookin' for new cookie receipes in that woman's magazine?"

"No, sir," I answer.

"Information on the latest diet?"

"Nah. I'm not really paying attention to what's on the pages, I confess."

"I feel sorry for them women," he says. "Got them cookie receipes and diet information in the same magazine. Must be terribly confusing."

I shut the magazine and study the cover. He also looks at the teasers. " 'New Ways to Surprise Your Husband in Bed,' " he says a little too loudly. "Hey, ladies, it's not that hard. We're surprised when you just say yes!" He laughs at his own joke.

Dr. Anderson comes into the waiting room. "I thought I recognized that laugh!" he says to Grandpa. He notices the bumps, frowns, and asks, "What have you got there?"

"That's what I'm here for," Grandpa tells him.

"Well, ask the nurse for a big black Sharpie marker and draw a circle around them. My eyesight is going to hell, and my nervous tremor is getting worse. But if you just draw me a few circles, I suspect we'll both be fine."

I must have looked alarmed because they both start laughing at me. "That one is so gullible," Grandpa says and gives me a wink. "You ready for me now?"

As a nurse approaches, Dr. Anderson says, "First, you get to let my nurse see how much pie you've been eating this fall. Sally, does our scale go up to three hundred?"

"Three hundred ninety-nine," she answers. "Beyond that we have to go next door to Dr. Reimer's scale."

"It's so handy having a vet next door," Dr. Anderson says. Grandpa follows Sally the nurse, and I wait.

Finally, he walks down the hall toward me. He gives me a reassuring smile, which I return, but I see something in his eyes I haven't seen in a long time: fragility. Suddenly I see him as he is now, in this moment—not the indestructible man I remember from ten to twenty years ago. And in this moment, he is fragile and scared. I realize I am the strong one now. It's my turn to take care of him. But as I realize how ill-equipped I am to be the strong one, I also get a small glimpse into what it must have been like for him when he was broken and asked to take care of me. I stand and wait for him.

"Come on, boy. You're going to help me pick out a Christmas present for my wife," he says without stopping. He just puts his arm on my back and guides me out with him. We get in the pickup. "They're going to call me in a couple days," he says, looking out the passenger-side window so I can't see his face. "Let's stop at the café first. If I'm going to drop some cash on your grandmother's Christmas present, I better have some food in my belly so I don't pass out."

I chuckle softly at how the more he tries to hide his nice side, the more he actually reveals it. "Sure thing, Grandpa."

MARA

The barnyard seems empty. The December steers have been shipped off. It is the way it is. I wish I could feel more at peace with it. This afternoon I watched them being loaded up and shipped off to die. It reminded me of saying good-bye to my dad for the last time. In the end he was shipped off to die, too.

But cows are cows, and people are people, right? Or are we

all sentient beings? Am I the only person who struggles with this?

DANIEL

While Mary Beth O'Callighan sings the last of "Ave Maria" in church, I remember the time Lance Grennan, Tim's younger brother, stood on the pew during one of her solos, plugged his ears, and yelled, "It hurts my ears! It hurts my ears!" We were the same age . . . maybe five. My parents giggled. I suspected everyone in the whole church secretly wanted to do the same thing.

When she finishes now, the altar boys bring out the wine and wafers for communion. Father McCleary says his bit, and the first row stands.

Grandma leans over Grandpa and me to whisper to Mara, "I'm sorry dear, but only Catholics can take communion."

"That's okay," Mara says. "I came prepared." She reaches into her purse and pulls out a silver flask and some Wheat Thins. She adds a slice of cheese to the Wheat Thin and pops it in her mouth. Then she takes a swig from her flask. "Jesus doesn't like exclusion." Our row stands and awkwardly walks in front of her as she prepares another cheese-and-cracker sandwich.

Tim, who sits behind her, taps her on the shoulder, and she turns around. From where I stand in the aisle, I hear him ask, "Hey, what you drinkin' there?"

"A lovely Chilean merlot," she answers.

"Mind if I have a hit of that?" he asks. She hands him the flask, and he takes a swig. Others watch in horror. Then Tim's row stands and joins us in line.

Grandma, Grandpa, and I take communion and return to Mara.

"So if the cracker is Jesus' body, what is the cheese?" I ask.

"Um . . . the Holy Spirit," she says with a smile. "It's all about the Trinity, Daniel."

"Right," I say.

Grandpa leans over me. "Psst! Hey, Mara, can I have some of that? I'm hungry, and that communion wine is not so tasty." Mara hands him the flask and makes him a cheese-and-cracker sandwich. He pops it in his mouth and takes a swig.

Grandma gives him a gentle punch and an embarrassed look.

Church is definitely more fun with Mara. I hold out my hand, and she gives me a cheese-and-cracker sandwich, too.

"To the Holy Spirit," I say.

"To the Holy Spirit," she echoes and pops another into her mouth.

EARL

You'll never guess who showed up at my goddamned door today. Tom O'Connor. Yup, Tom O'Connor trying to save my none-of-his-damn-business soul. Word must be spreadin' or somethin'. He asked me—right to my face, mind you—"Earl, have you accepted the Lord Jesus Christ as your savior?"

"Tom," I replied, "Jesus and I talk all the time. In fact, He told me you were comin'. He told me to tell you He's tired of all you know-it-alls preachin' his teachings like some kind of goddamned used car salesman. He also said God has a special Heaven for y'all for two reasons: One, so you can watch your life over and over and realize how stupid and pompous you were; two, Heaven wouldn't be Heaven to the rest of us if we had to hang out with obnoxious folk like you." I shut the door.

You know, as I see it, there are two kinds of folks who act

nice. The first kind acts nice because they are nice. The others, though, the others act nice because they're tryin' to score God points. Now, I must confess that at times I feel sorry for them, stressin' out about whether God likes 'em enough, but you know, those folks just really get on my nerves. Seem insincere to me.

Tom tryin' to save my soul, as if he has some God-like powers, as if he's better than the rest of us. Tom can blow it out his ass. My redemption is between me and God and no one else.

EDITH

Mara and I exchange Christmas gifts in the sauna. I give her muslin bags filled with lavender to take with her to her grandmother's, and she gives me a bottle of pure rose essential oil. We are two deliciously fragrant women.

The sauna is wonderfully hot and filled with the floral scents. When I shut my eyes, I can imagine it's actually one of those late afternoons in the summer, right before a thunderstorm when the air is still and humid and you stick to everything, when it's too hot to move, and all a person can do is sit on the porch swing, drink iced tea, and hope for rain. When I open my eyes, I'm relieved to see snow outside.

"It's time," I say.

"That's a copy," Mara replies with that spirited smile I love so much.

With that we bolt for the door, dive in the snow, make snow angels, and giggle. Zeus gets really excited, running circles around us, letting out a few barks to match our shrieks and eventually making dog snow angels next to Mara. His barks set off Harvey, who begins to grunt and run back and forth in his pen, seemingly dying to be part of the game. I don't think I'd want a four-hundred-pound hog making hog snow angels next to me, though.

While we flap our arms and legs, Mara asks, "Edith, what has been your favorite age so far?"

I think about this and laugh a little. I don't think I could've realized when I was Mara's age that I would feel pretty much the same at my age. Perhaps I live my life with a little more grace now. I don't have an answer for her. "You know, Mara, every age I've ever been has seemed like the perfect age to be."

She sits up, looks in my eyes, and says, "What a wonderful answer."

❧

I step out of the shower and crack the door to let some air in. Through the crack I hear Mara ask Earl, "Earl, will you be okay if I go?"

"Oh, sure," he says.

"Will you be here when I get back?" I bristle.

"I think so," he answers. "We'll slop Harvey. He's kinda growin' on me."

"Don't let the word out," Daniel says, "but he secretly brings back doggie bags from the café on Saturdays." Daniel laughs.

"Do you know how much ridicule I'd receive if anyone knew I was bringin' home treats for the infamous hog? But he sure does get excited about pancakes," Earl confesses.

Mara laughs.

"Hey, Earl, my Gram's been visualizing a horse for me. Her visions always manifest. Do you mind if I bring a horse back here from Gram's?"

"I don't know what all that 'visions' and 'manifest' crap you're talking about is all about, but if you wanna bring back a horse of your own, that's fine with me." For a minute he sounds like his old cranky self again, and for a minute I can pretend that my whole world isn't turning upside down.

"Thanks, Earl," she says tenderly.

❦

Mara is nearly done packing her pickup. We watch her call her dog up into the cab and figure she is about to take off. The three of us walk out to say good-bye.

"Do you have chains?" Earl asks.

"Yes, sir," she replies.

"I packed some snacks for the road," I say and hand her a paper sack.

"Wow! Thanks, Edith," she says.

She looks Daniel right in the eye and says, "Merry Christmas." She hugs me. She says, "Thank you for everything," as she hugs Earl. Then she gets in her pickup and goes.

MARA

I can't think of the Christmas season at Gram's house without thinking of Pizza Hut. Gram didn't really know what to do when I became a vegetarian, so we just ordered pizza from then on so we could each get what we wanted. Tonight, though, Gram and I are going upscale—Cucina Cucina. We eat elephant garlic and focaccia bread and watch people. Gram uses this opportunity to try to find me a boyfriend.

"How about him?" she asks, raising her eyebrows up and down.

"Oh, please, Gram, he's gay."

"How do you know?" she challenges.

"Um . . . could it be the way he has his arm around the guy next to him?" I get smart.

"It could be his brother," she says, defending her point.

"It's not his brother," I state firmly.

Then we get quiet to overhear three couples in their late forties joke and tease each other about theme night, which I'm getting clearer involves acting out bedroom fantasies. Overhearing this with my Gram makes me a little uncomfortable.

She leans over and asks me quietly, "Are you listening to this?"

"Yes," I reply, sounding a little embarrassed.

"That's the secret to a long and happy marriage."

You can only imagine the look on my face.

❧

Since driving with Gram is sort of like driving with Mr. Magoo, I am driving, and she gives me directions. Eventually, she guides me into a gravel driveway. A woman comes out of the house and waves at us. I park and we get out.

"Mara, this is Leslie. She's in my Miracles Group." Gram meets in a nearby café with a few other women once a week to study *A Course in Miracles*; she calls them her Miracles Group. The café used to be a bar called The Alibi, and Uncle Bob likes to tease her about hanging out at The Alibi.

"Your grandma told us how much you wanted a horse, so we visualized one for you the last few months, and look what showed up!" She gestures toward a chestnut gelding; it is about eighteen hands and has a crescent-moon-shaped mark on his face. I'm guessing he's a thoroughbred.

"My friends raise race horses. This guy had a little injury on the track that won't affect him for pleasure purposes but will keep him from winning. Since he's not good for breeding, they just gave him to me. He's three, quite hot, but sweet. I don't think he's been outside a stable or track much, so you'll need to help him adjust to new environments."

"Oh, wow," I manage to get out in those moments when I

can't seem to get words out of my mouth. "He's gorgeous!" I'm finally able to say. "Thank you so much!" I walk over to blow up his nose and let him blow up mine.

ᎠᎯᏁᎥᎬᏞ

Grandpa and I sit in recliners watching the national rodeo finals in Las Vegas that he taped for me.

"See that guy?" he struggles to get out. Talking has gotten difficult for him. He points at the screen. "You were better than that guy."

I know I'm supposed to feel flattered, but I feel guilty and crawl back inside myself.

"I'm sorry I let you down, Grandpa," I say.

He looks at me a little surprised and says, "Shoot, you didn't let me down. Probably saved my marriage, that's what you did." He goes back to watching the screen.

I think back to my own bull-riding days.

On the ranch I felt invisible, but as I grew older and learned just how much weakness had no place in this world, I felt grateful for being relatively invisible. But there in the safety of whatever county fair arena I happened to be in, I drank up their attention. We all knew how to deal with each other. And there, because of the brutality of the sport, more softness in other areas seemed okay. There, men pray with each other before the event, and older men will pat you on the shoulder and give you fatherly advice. It was a family of sorts, but a safe one, one that didn't get too close, one where the rules were clear and the topic of conversation was always the same.

It was a relief to me to have an expression for the turmoil I lived with. My life looked so quiet and still to anyone watching, but in the moments when a bull was whipping me around—and

I swear I could feel the molecules in my body separate according to atomic weight as if I were in a primitive centrifuge—in those moments, I felt like I was finally being honest about what my inner world was like. And when I'd smack the dirt, only to have the bull run right over my back and the numbness would rush over me . . . in those moments, I felt a sort of relief at finally having my physical reality match the reality in my heart. And when I got up and saw the relieved look on Grandpa Earl's face, I finally got the acknowledgment for living through hell that I had wanted from him since I was eight.

On the screen we watch a bull rider get tossed off a giant Brahma like a rag doll. The announcer, Donny Gay, a former bull-riding champion, walks us through the slow-motion replay, and when the cowboy hits the dirt, Gay shouts, "Ker-splat!"

Grandpa chuckles and then, without looking at me, says, "I sure do love you, boy."

At first I can't believe what I just heard. But he sneaks a look at me out of the corner of his eye, and I say, "I love you, too, Grandpa."

This is it, I know—my last days with Grandpa—and I can't waste them. Still, we go back to watching bull riding and pretending like nothing happened. Maybe little moments of truth are enough.

MARA

In my dream Emmylou Harris sings "Waltz Across Texas Tonight," and Earl shows up in Gram's backyard to dance with me.

"Now don't get waltzes confused with the fox-trot like you always do. There's no quick-quick anywhere. Get it straight, Red."

"Stop crankin' at me already!" I reply, smiling. We start dancing. "Hey, what do you think of my new horse?" I gesture at the paddock.

"I think you better get yourself a good ladder and a solid helmet."

"Yeah, I'll get right on that," I say without meaning it. "Hey, Earl? How's everything going?"

"Well, it sure is nice to be out of my body, I can tell you that much. Now why don't you stop talkin' for all of two minutes and just enjoy the rest of this dance with me?"

Then we dance and dance and float up into the starry night sky.

EDITH

"Help me up," Earl croaks out. When he's on his feet, he makes raspy noises as he catches his breath. He puts his arms around me. "Sing me 'The Tennessee Waltz,'" he requests tenderly.

I choke back my tears and sing softly as we sort of sway. "Don't go," I softly whisper to him, my head on his shoulder where he can't see my tears, but undoubtedly he feels them soak through his nightshirt. I lift my head to look into his eyes and see an expression that shows his heart is surely breaking. Suddenly, I feel ashamed of my selfishness, my wanting to keep him here despite his pain. "I'm sorry. That wasn't very fair now, was it?"

He purses his lips together and gently shakes his head, looking at me with empathy. "I won't be very far behind you." I try to smile through my tears. He replies by holding my head so that we are cheek to cheek, and I feel his tears mix with mine.

"I'll be waiting for you there," he manages to get out.

DANIEL

I open my eyes, stare up at my model airplane suspended by fishing line, and for a brief moment feel disoriented in time. It's Christmas. It's Christmas morning! And then I remember that I'm twenty-eight and that my grandfather is dying, and that flash of childhood excitement drains out of me like old motor oil.

I go downstairs and start a fire to warm up the house. The crackle of the fire relieves the deafening silence of the house. I take a tangerine off the mantel and peel it. This Christmas reminds me of the first one without my parents. My grandparents tried to carry on so that I wouldn't lose faith in Santa, but all of our hearts were as heavy as lead. I believe we all snuck off to our corners many times that day to cry.

There is no doubt all of our hearts will be heavy today, too. It's our last Christmas together.

I go to the kitchen, put orange juice and Grandma's cinnamon rolls with the orange zest icing on a tray. I carry the tray up to my grandparents' door, stop, and listen. I hear voices, so I knock softly and open the door slowly.

"Daniel!" Grandma says. "Merry Christmas!"

"We're all together," Grandpa says, choked up.

Oh, God, it's going to be a hard day, but I'm so glad I'm here. I hug each of them. When Grandma excuses herself to go to the bathroom, Grandpa says, "Get her present, will you? It's in the pocket of my wool coat." I find it and bring it to him.

When she returns, he presents her with the small shiny red package. She's genuinely surprised. "Oh, Earl. How did you pull this off?" She looks at me.

"Don't look at me," I say. "This was all him."

"I planned ahead," he says.

She unwraps the paper so slowly that I know she must be

very aware that this is the last gift from him she'll ever receive. She opens the small cardboard box to reveal a little velvet box and blinks back tears. She opens the velvet box and stares at the diamond ring for a moment before she puts it on next to her wedding band. "Oh, Earl," she says through tears, "oh, Earl." She kisses him on the lips, and he wraps his arms around her.

"Merry Christmas, beloved Edith," he says. And it hits me. It hits me hard. She is about to lose him, and he's about to leave her—and still they love hard, they love big. They love each other with everything they have. And if they can love like this under these circumstances, what's my excuse? "I've got something for you, too, boy," he says, and he reaches into his nightstand drawer and pulls out a gold pocket watch. "It was my father's," he says. "It still works. Don't get it wet."

"Thank you, Grandpa," I say as I study it in disbelief. I wasn't allowed to even touch it as a child. "I promise I'll take good care of it."

"I know you will," he says. I lean over to give him a little hug, too.

"I have a little something for you, too," I say. During Mara's last dance lesson with Grandpa, I snapped a few pictures, and then when my grandparents thought I had gone to bed, I snuck down and shot two more. It was the first one that was a keeper. They are looking deep into each other's eyes as they dance. Grandma has dried roses in her hair. It's the passion, though, the passion on their faces, the passion in their eyes that makes the photograph. I met Mara after school one day and printed it with the ancient photography equipment in the old art room where she works. I blew it up as big as I could, eighteen by twenty-four, and I spared no expense to frame it right. I slip back to my bedroom and pull it out from under my bed without ripping the wrapping paper. I carry it back to them, hopeful that they'll love it as much as I do. I hold it up next to Grandpa. "Open it together," I say.

Grandma reaches over, looks at Grandpa, and asks, "Ready?"

"On your mark, get set, go!" he says, and they tear into it like little kids.

And then they look at it. I study their faces carefully for approval, but instead I see their hearts break. Grandma touches it tenderly. "Daniel, we're speechless," she finally says. "This is a beautiful, beautiful gift."

Grandpa's chin quivers, and he blinks rapidly to fight back more tears. "Look how beautiful your grandmother is. How did a chump like me ever get so lucky?"

"Put it there," Grandma instructs me. "Put it right there so we can look at it." I set it on the dresser and lean it up against the wall, just like she asked.

"I have a little surprise for the two of you, too," she says, "but it's an experience rather than a thing. Daniel, will you help me with this?" She leads the way to the door we never open, to my father's childhood bedroom. On the floor near the door is an old projector, which I pick up, and a box containing reels of film, which she picks up. We carry them back to their bedroom. "Put it on that chair, will you?" She takes some pictures and a mirror off the wall and sets them on the dresser, plugs in the projector, and loads the first strip of film. I had no idea these existed. I turn off the lights and watch with them.

We watch reel after reel of Christmases past, most of them before I was born, and two after I was. For two hours I watch my father as a child, running around the yard, riding a horse, playing with an old dog, unwrapping a rifle, getting ready for graduation in his cap and gown, and riding bulls just like me. In the flickering light I see my grandmother weep as she watches, while my grandfather shakes his head slowly, sadly, except for brief moments when something my father did still makes him smile.

I see my father grow up, his life begun and almost over so quickly, and I see my grandparents starting around my age mature until they become grandparents. I glance over at them again. Their wrinkled faces are even more dramatic in the flickering light. It's over so quickly, I think. It's all over so quickly.

I see both my father and my mom get out of that old green pickup, my father with an armload of presents and my mother carrying me, and Grandma runs to hug them and greet them. Look how happy we were, all five of us, all five of us together for that brief moment in time. As each year of my life passes, the fraction of my life when we were all together dwindles— one-half, one-third, three-eighths, and in four more years, just a quarter.

I watch myself stick my hands in my first birthday cake. Everyone laughs. I can see how much they all love me. I can see how it was supposed to be. And then tears stream steadily down my face. I wish I could touch their image on the wall and touch them. I wish I could hear their voices. I wish I could feel them hug me. All of it overwhelms me like a surge of water so big that it could crumble anything in its path.

And then I feel my grandmother's hand on my back. She knows. She feels it, too. In my peripheral vision I see flickering light reflect on their tears, too. Grandma takes my hand in her right and Grandpa's in her left, transforming us from three dammed-up reservoirs into one free-flowing river.

❧

On New Year's Day I stop in the hallway with a glass in my hand to watch my grandparents for a moment. Grandpa's breathing is clearly an effort. His lumps are huge. He shuts his eyes tightly. The pain is evident on his face.

Grandma holds his head up and tries to bring a straw to his lips so he can sip some water. "There you go," she says gently.

Grandpa takes a few sips, releases the straw, and turns his head. Grandma sets his head down.

I speak up. "Hey, Grandpa. Mara made you this. Some kind of juice. Has ginger in it. Says it will help your stomach and help the inflammation in your neck. Smells good."

Grandpa looks at me with a pained expression. I walk over, sit in a nearby chair, and hand the juice to Grandma, who offers it to Grandpa. He winces and turns his head away from the straw. Grandma sets the juice down on the bedside table. Grandpa looks toward the window and back at me. I know what he's thinking.

"I bought one of those solar-powered trough heaters so the livestock water won't freeze anymore," I say.

He nods.

"I'm taking good care of everything," I assure him.

He nods again. Grandma looks at me with appreciation, knowing it's hard for Grandpa not to worry about the ranch.

"Doc Anderson called. He's coming out today to give you something for the pain."

Grandpa nods again, and a couple tears escape. He turns his head away so I won't see.

"Okay, Grandpa. I'm here for you." I give his hand a squeeze. He continues to look away as more tears break through his dam.

❧

I get in the pickup with the hopper on it that doles out up to one ton of high-protein range cubes. Grandpa has it all figured out so that each animal should get two pounds. The hopper has a calculator attached to it that counts the revolutions. Each revolution distributes four pounds.

First, I go out to the two-year-olds. We keep them within a half mile of the barn so we can get to them easily when they calve. Two-year-olds have smaller bodies. It's not uncommon for a calf's head or shoulders to get stuck when the two-year-olds calve for the first time. Sometimes two-year-olds have their baby and are scared of it. They want to love it, but they don't know what to do. I open the gate and drive in. They see me and start to gather. I hit the gas and outrun them. They chase me and string out so that when I turn around and drive back toward them, dropping pounds of cake, they're nice and spread out so they can get their share. I check the counter. Fifty-four revolutions for two hundred head. Very close.

Next, I go to the pasture with the three-year-olds. They're still growing, and they shed their teeth this year. Grandpa doesn't put them in with the older herd just yet because the boss cows who have a little age on them fight off the young, timid ones. As the three-year-olds' permanent teeth come in, they sure don't need to be competing with boss cows for food. My counter is up to 106 revolutions. I'm right on target.

The older herd is divided into two groups. Grandpa doesn't like to have more than four hundred head or so in a group. These older heifers are the farthest out. They are pros at calving. Grandpa keeps them until they drop since they are the best moms. Every year, though, he culls one-fourth of the herd, and there's always some older ones in that group. Their teeth eventually get worn down to nothing, or sometimes they just disappear. You gotta have good teeth to make it through a winter. I feed them and return to the barn to refill the hopper.

Then I go to the bulls. We've got about 270 bulls now, one bull for every 20 cows or so, plus a couple extra. They fight each other and get hurt. We always cull the older bulls. By the time they are seven or eight, their libido has gone down. They often have a crippled knee or shoulder that keeps them from traveling to breed cows. The younger bulls are a force to be reckoned with. They're dangerous. Some of those two-year-old bulls can breed 40 cows a year. We put the yearling bulls with the yearling cows so they can all figure it out together.

I feed the yearling heifers last, since they get a few extras to get some size on them.

Then I load hay onto the truck we use to distribute it and make the same rounds with it.

Grandma and Grandpa need me here. I wish they didn't, but they do. Even though Mara will be back tomorrow, she can't do all this all winter and teach. Maybe Grandma will sell the ranch after Grandpa passes. I don't know how it will all work out, but they took me in when I needed help, and now it's my turn to help them. I go home and call the captain to tell him I won't be able to be on his snow crab crew. I tell him that I'll check in with him in April to let him know if I can make it for another salmon season, but that I'm hopeful I will. Most of calving will happen in March. In May, though, branding, castration, and vaccinations need to be done. How will they pull that off? Maybe Grandma could hire a crew for that. It only takes about three days. And in the summer I think Grandma and Mara can handle the silage with a little help from Whitey.

There's got to be a way. I really don't want to stay here.

MARA

In my dream, I'm a deer this time. I walk through the door at the back of the McRae house, walk up the stairs, and turn into a woman. I'm wearing the buckskin angel wings I received from my Angel, the ones with the fringe at the bottom and some eagle feathers tied to a few strands of fringe. I don't know what Earl will think of my wings, so I wrap them around me when I talk to Earl so he'll think they are a hippie shawl instead.

I watch Earl sleep. He's having trouble getting air because that lump is pushing on his larynx. The expression on his sleeping face is not one of rest but of pain.

"Earl," I say gently. He comes out of his deep sleep and into the spiritual REM with me. "Earl, how are you doing?"

"I want to go Home," he replies, tired.

"Want me to take you there?" I volunteer.

"Yup."

"Should we invite Edith so she knows how to find you?"

"I think that'd be nice," he says like I'm an idiot for asking such an obvious question.

"Edith," I say, "Earl's ready to go Home now. Would you like to go with me to drop him off so you know where he is?"

She nods, and with that the three of us float up, up into the sky. When we get to the level where we feel our spirits expand and become part of everything, I know we are very close. We expand into the source of all love and ascend even higher. Here, a soul is filled with immense peace. I hope this helps Edith let go. Even though we're not quite there yet, we can smell roses, and Edith and Earl seem to be savoring it. Earl's celestial guardians come down to show him the rest of the way Home, so he stops us and gives us a look that says go on back now.

Edith and I stop while he continues to ascend with his guardians; but before he is out of sight, he turns and blows Edith a kiss.

Edith squeezes my hand as she watches Earl float out of sight. She doesn't want to return to the ranch, but we both know it's not her time. I carry Edith back to her bed to finish her sleep, hoping she will remember the peace she felt near Heaven.

EDITH

His silence woke me.

I roll over and face him, then touch his face. It's neither warm nor cold. It's something in between, which feels appropriate, like the transition it is. Something in between, like my acceptance of the situation.

I can smell that in the moments following his soul's departure, his body had soiled the bed. I wish I could lie here with his body and say my good-byes, but the smell repels me and I get up. I'm not ready to walk away, though, so I sit in the chair next to the bed. I sit and just stare at him. I stare at his eyebrows that had grown longer over the years. I stare at all the ways he had changed over the years and at the ways he had stayed the same. He always had a strong jaw. I liked that strong jaw. I study the wrinkles in his face and try to read them like a story—our story. And though I know our story had a happy ending, I wish I could read more evidence that it had been a happier story in general. I see pain. I see contentment. I see determination. I always admired that about him—his determination.

I stare at his body like it is my own, and I stare at his body like it is foreign. I know his body perhaps better than my own, and yet with his spirit gone, his body begins to look strangely unfamiliar to me. It looks like a house I used to live in but don't anymore: vacant but familiar. The floor plan is known so well that I could walk it in the dark, but all the things that made it mine are missing.

I know I am supposed to call someone, but I'm not ready for them to come and invade the sacred space I shared with

Earl. I am not ready for them to invade Earl's sacred body like it was a broken car. I know it is just his body, but I loved that body. I still do. I've loved it for sixty years, and once they take it away, I won't ever see it again. I won't ever see him again. And in the same breath I know this isn't Earl anymore.

It's been so hard to see Earl trapped inside that body, that body that had turned on him, turned on us; the body I had loved; the body that gave me Sam. I think of how he suffered for weeks now—weeks where every moment was agony, where every day was torture. And though you'd think I might, I don't exactly feel relief. Relief isn't quite accurate. Maybe release is.

I try to reconcile the conflict between my attachment to Earl and my gladness not to watch him suffer anymore. But there is no reconciliation; all the fragmented parts of my broken heart cry out different things.

I stare at him and try to etch it in my mind so I won't forget anything, and then I think, Why? Why do I want so hard to remember him dead? So I try to remember him alive, to remember every detail of the nights we danced recently, every detail of the day we met, every detail about our wedding, of birthday parties, of Christmases. But the more I try to remember, the more the memories run from me. And as the fear of being unable to remember washes over me, I am able to remember even less.

I know I am supposed to call someone, but I want to make sure that he is so dead that no one could possibly revive him and make him suffer more.

I stare and I stare, and after a while the body doesn't look like Earl to me anymore. It just looks like a body, ashen and empty and more and more unfamiliar as each moment passes. And with each moment that passes, I feel him slip further and further away.

I know that in reality I said my good-byes, but before I leave the room, I say again, "Thank you, Earl. From the bottom of my heart, thank you."

And then as I walk away from him, walk down the hall toward the stairs, it seems real and no longer like a strange dream. It seems real like a kick in the stomach, real like having to call someone to take the only body my body has ever loved, real like severing, real like thunderstorms of sad tears, storms that rack my body and shake the house.

WINTER

DANIEL

Grandma is in terrible shape. She hasn't eaten for days. I look at her, so fragile, and realize she is all that remains of my family.

Mara draws Grandma a bath in the old claw-foot tub and pours a drop of rose oil in it. "When you grieve for him, it's really important to picture white light around him. We'll be back in twenty minutes. Please wait for us to return before you get out. I don't want you to fall." She leaves Grandma alone in the bathroom.

"She needs to scream and howl," Mara says to me, "but I know she won't do it with us in the house. Would you like to go for a walk or a ride, or if you like, we could just hang out at the Church of the Dog?"

I don't remember much about our ride except the warmth and smell of the horse as we rode bareback and the eerie sound of my grandmother screaming in the distance.

EDITH

Sometimes I think I'll surely die of heartbreak, and then there are moments when Earl's departure doesn't seem real to me. I appreciate these moments of detachment and watching the time like I could take or leave it. I appreciate these moments like other people might appreciate a trip to the Bahamas.

Isabel Moloney caught me during one of these moments today when she dropped a Jell-O off for us. When she left, I had to laugh a little. Once, before Earl left the church, Isabel asked for his help with some household repair, and he saw her kitchen. Suffice it to say, Isabel wasn't much of a housekeeper—cats on the counter and such. That didn't sit well with Earl. Said he knew where their paws had been. Anyway, after that, Earl wouldn't eat anything she brought to the church potlucks that I dragged him to.

So when Isabel dropped her Jell-O by, well, Daniel and I knew what we had to do. He turned on the garbage disposal, and I called up to the sky, "This one's for you, Earl!" as I dumped it in the sink. Then Daniel gave me a high-five, and we laughed for a minute, something between a laugh and a cry, really.

Sure was thoughtful of Isabel, though, wasn't it?

DANIEL

The last time I was here was a few days after my parents' funeral. We drove up to the church. Grandpa dropped off Grandma and me and then went to park the car. Grandma paused to look at the church before starting up the path, holding my hand.

I didn't budge. She gave my hand a little tug. "C'mon," she said.

"*No!*" I stammered, more afraid than angry. She looked at

me for a minute, her fatigue obvious. "We need to turn to God right now."

But as far as I was concerned, that church wasn't God. That church was a building I sat in for what seemed like forever, looking at two boxes containing what was left of my parents. I wasn't about to go back in there. *"No!"* I told her again, more freaked out and more adamant.

"We are going to church," she told me firmly and started up the walk holding my hand again.

"No!" I screamed and broke free. I ran. I ran wildly and blindly for two blocks and then across Main Street, over the bridge that goes to the school yard, around the fence, and down to the creek, where I hid under the bridge. Maybe I blacked out, maybe I fell asleep, or maybe I just don't remember those ten hours.

What I do remember is a police officer named Dawson shining his light on me. "C'mon out, son," he said in a low, gentle voice. Turns out some kids had noticed me there and told when someone asked if they had seen me.

"I'm not your son! You're not my dad! My dad is dead! My parents are dead!" I screamed at him. He looked down, and I screamed at him again, "They're dead!"

"I know," he said quietly. "They were my friends."

"How could they die? I need them! I need them!" I told him, bewildered and confused.

"I know," he said and exhaled loudly, "but your grandparents will take good care of you."

"But I need *them*," I cried. "I need them! Don't they know I need them?" I started sobbing and wedged myself higher in the space between the creek slope and the footbridge.

I heard footsteps running over the bridge and then saw Grandma and Grandpa squatting beside the officer. Suddenly I felt very calm, and I said to my grandparents, "I'm never going to see them again."

"We'll see them in Heaven," Grandma told me.

"Then why did the priest say we had to pray for their souls to get in? How do you know they made it?" I asked, suddenly all rational.

"Father McCleary is full of shit," Grandpa began, to the horror of Grandma and the shock of the officer. "Of course they're in Heaven. There's no question. Now let's go home and get something to eat. I'm hungry."

And so I came out, and Grandma and Grandpa held each of my hands as the three of us walked off calmly and quietly back to the car as if nothing had happened. But from then on Grandpa and I stayed home from church when Grandma went.

It was the last time I ever felt anything passionately. Twenty years later I am here again, holding my grandmother's hand as we walk up the path. I want to go run under the bridge again, but I don't. This time I don't run. I hold my grandmother's soft hand, and I try to be strong for her.

I sit in the same pew with Grandma, who is white and shaking, and I put my arm around her, shut my eyes, and imagine myself like the boat I worked on, floating on the ocean on winter nights in fifty-foot waves. There were times it looked like our boat was no match for the enormous sea. I just sit there and think about floating, floating in any storm, floating through anything even when it feels so much bigger than me.

Every once in a while, something Father McCleary says catches my ear, something that defies common sense, and I hear Grandpa say, "Father McCleary is full of shit."

MARA

It's so hard to see Edith like this. It's like I can't reach her. And somewhere along the line my psychic protective force shield disintegrated, and now I can't tell her feelings from my own. I'm just absorbing everything.

The small steers and feeder heifers get picked up tomorrow. I'm trying not to think about that, either. Each one will be about eight hundred dollars, much needed to sustain Edith. I know that. It just feels like death is everywhere, like it's draping over all of us like a lead apron at the dentist's office. I can't seem to shut it out. I'm going to make an effort not to be here when the truck arrives.

Times like these all I can do to stay sane is curl up in a hot bath, read *Organic Gardening*, and dream of warmer days. I dream of feeling warm dirt between my toes and of eating tomatoes off the vine, warmed in the sun. The Church of the Dog doesn't have hot water, so I go to the McRaes' to bathe every night, and once a week I indulge in a bath.

I decided that everything I plant in my garden next spring will be purple to represent the spirit chakra: lilacs, irises— particularly the ones that smell like grape popsicles!—pansies, hyacinths, petunias, bachelor's buttons, forget-me-nots, lobelia, lupine, wisteria, clematis, and lavender, especially lavender.

Edith has me hooked on lavender. Last September we cut many of her remaining lavender blossoms, sewed muslin bags, and put the lavender inside them. One floats in the tub now, infusing the bathwater with fragrance. Edith is my teacher of simple pleasures.

I pick up a seed catalog and mark another page. Did you know that in addition to purple vegetables like eggplant and red cabbage, which looks purple to me, you can purchase purple varieties of almost any vegetable? I take a highlighter and highlight Purple Passion asparagus, All Blue potatoes (which really look purple), Purple Pod pole beans, Purple Beauty peppers, Rainbow corn, and Purple Ruffles basil.

I think I'll grow grapes, too. Perhaps I'll even try making wine. Might help the longevity of my teaching career.

I put down the seed catalog, close my eyes, and dream of the brightness of summer, bright flowers, and bright sky. I dream of lazy days, of lying down and watching white puffy clouds drift through the sapphire blue sky. I dream of long days heating the sage so that the warm, windy nights smell fragrant and medicinal. I breathe deep, inhaling lavender, trying to clear myself, clear my mind.

I give up, pick up my *Organic Gardening* magazine again, and read an article on edible flowers. Seems like a waste to eat something so beautiful, if you ask me.

DANIEL

I remember sitting here in this tub as a boy, the heavy steam filling the room, making it hard to breathe. Here, I would sit by myself, and it would hit me how truly alone I was. Sometimes I could hear sounds of Grandma working in the kitchen or Grandpa outside in the barnyard, and I would fantasize about running to them, jumping in their arms, and breaking down. They would stroke my hair and tell me everything would be okay. But I didn't, and they didn't. Instead, I just ran for the window whenever my lungs got so tight I couldn't breathe. I'd stick my head out and suck in a long, arduous breath.

People like to say that time heals all wounds, but I don't believe it. I remember once when Grandpa took me firewood cutting, we looked at the rings of the tree together, and he pointed out the years where there was drought and the years where there was fire. So while time allowed for new growth that hid the scars of the past, those scars were still there, inside the tree and part of the tree. I think about how I'm like that tree.

I can hear Grandma in the kitchen. I want to get out of the tub and put my arms around her. But I don't. Instead, I get out, open the window, and breathe deeply.

MARA

In my dream I'm at the Grand Canyon with Zeus. Actually, we're floating above it.

"Oh! I was hoping you'd meet me here!" I hear to my left, and I turn to see Adam.

"Hey, nice to see you!" I greet him and smile.

"Wanna fly through the canyon?" he proposes.

"Oh, yeah!" I answer, and then the three of us go speeding through the canyon, flying down to touch the river, and back up halfway around the corners, on and on. Even Zeus is smiling.

And then it's time to get up and prepare for another workday.

❧

All of a sudden Kelli seems to have discovered herself as an artist. I noticed her picking up speed with her charcoal strokes, which I like to see. Speed makes a piece look full of energy and movement. I wanted to see what she would do if she worked big, so in class today I taped big pieces of butcher paper to the wall. She looked uncomfortably around the room and asked if she could come back after school and try.

Now here she is.

"Can I turn up your music?" she asks.

"You like Tori Amos, too?"

"Is that who this is?"

"Yep. It's an old one," I tell her. "Turn it up as loud as you want." I begin to unload the kiln while she gets her supplies and gets to work.

Kelli is also a redhead, but the very rich coppery kind. She has no freckles, a delicate nose, and brown eyes. She is built much smaller than me. She moves like a bulldog as she walks over to the boom box, turns it up, and approaches the wall where the paper hangs. Then she just stands in front of the big paper for a moment, intimidated perhaps. I can see the back of her shoulders rise and fall as she takes a big breath. I focus my attention back on the kiln so that I don't feed her pressure with the energy of my interest.

I pull out a slab pot of Audra's that looks like something in a Georgia O'Keeffe painting. The bold sides have a gentle curve out and then in. That girl has great style. I like her art better than my own.

Next, I take out Brandon's creation—an abstract sculpture with excellent balance. In parts of it I think I see screaming faces, but I'm not sure. I wonder what he'll do with it next. I might suggest turning it into a multimedia sculpture by adding some metal elements.

I pull out some ugly pinch pots and coil pots. There is something endearing about them, about their awkwardness and imperfection. In the imperfections I see something genuine—hope perhaps, hope that they can become the artist they want to become. It takes so much courage to start anything from the beginning and to be patient with yourself as you learn. It takes strength to keep trying when the results of your efforts are so unsatisfactory and it's not clear what you need to do to get different results. The same could be said whether it's creating art or creating life. The simple act of not giving up is true success.

I take the warped cone out of the hole and replace it with a new one. Then I begin to load the greenware. I handle the unfired clay very gently. I keep a fat pinch pot on the shelf. Its weight tells me there is still enough moisture inside that it would blow up in the kiln. I load a few small slab pots and then pick up one of Liz's vases. It has bold, curvy lines—great lines—but then I notice her vase has a couple extra holes. Dammit. Well, I can't be manufacturing bongs for kids, so I "accidentally" drop the "vase" and watch it break into pieces. Too bad. I really liked the lines.

When I glance back at Kelli, I can't believe what I see. She has filled two papers and is working on the third. She has drawn a pregnant woman on each, and each has a small crucifix behind her head. I suppose she's drawing the Madonna. Her fast strokes have given each woman a lot of life, and yet despite their size, there is still something delicate about them, something vulnerable. I walk over to her but stay a little farther back, and she turns to watch my reaction carefully. Tears well up in my eyes, and I sort of shake my head in disbelief. "Oh my God, Kelli. These are brilliant. These are really brilliant." I look in her eyes and nod a little.

There is an interesting moment when young people are confronted with their own brilliance. Very few embrace it right away. Most can't believe they are brilliant, but as they continue to look at the evidence, it gets harder to deny. Then there is a moment when you can see them consider the responsibility that comes with brilliance, and it scares them. They take a step back and want to deny their brilliance for a new reason. Occasionally, young people walk away from their talent at that moment, but most decide to step up. Then there is a final moment where I see relief, relief that they are really good enough, relief that there is something truly unique and special about them. I watch Kelli experience all those moments in the space of ten seconds. She smiles. She is proud of herself. I give her a couple pats on the back of her shoulder before walking back to the kiln.

I wonder about what the Madonna means to her, if that is in fact what she was intending to draw, and I think about how easy it is to underestimate the spiritual depth of teenagers. They can hide those parts of themselves so well. I wonder if Kelli has words for the content of her artwork, but that question is too personal to ask, so I don't.

EDITH

I breathe in deeply, holding his favorite shirt, the green and tan flannel one he wore five days out of seven, to my face. Oh, what a relief it is to smell his smell. But just as fast as the relief comes, it is replaced with the feeling of beng kicked in the stomach when I realize it's just a shirt, not him, and that I won't ever see him again on Earth. I feel a little panicked today because the smell isn't as strong as I remember it being a couple weeks ago. I know I'm supposed to give all this away to Goodwill or something, but I just can't—not yet, anyway. Not as long as his smell still lingers on them.

I confess I took one of his shirts, buttoned it around his pillow, and slept on it the first month after he died. I didn't change the sheets, either. Then everything began to smell like me, so I went ahead and washed it all.

I wonder how many other widows sit in their closets smelling clothes. Probably more than we'd guess.

My mother didn't, though. When Dad died, she had his closet cleaned out the next day. It wasn't that she didn't love him—I know she loved him passionately. Maybe all the re-

minders hurt her too much. Or maybe instead of a slow, tortur-
ous transition into accepting widowhood, maybe she thought
she could have a quick-severing one, get it over with and begin
healing. I don't know. I do know us kids weren't ready for it,
though. Some hadn't even accepted that Dad wasn't coming
back, and those of us who had weren't ready to let go. Mom's
willingness to let go of Dad's things was interpreted by some
of my brothers and sisters to mean that she did not love him.
I don't know how they could have thought that. To this day
two still haven't forgiven her. Families go a little nuts after one
member dies, don't you think?

I'm glad no one is here who wants to throw out Earl's things.
I pick out his wedding day suit, take the jacket off the hook,
and hold it like a dance partner.

We were married in the summer of 1947. My sisters and I
picked flowers that morning to put in the church and to make
my bouquet. Mom had made a beautiful two-tier white cake,
one small circle sitting right on top of a larger circle, and a
single pink rose was stuck into the top of the cake. Simple.
Elegant. Our little reception was in the churchyard. There were
little children playing tag and friends sitting on blankets enjoying a picnic. John O'Kelly brought his fiddle. First he played a
waltz for us, and Earl waltzed me around the churchyard. After
that, John picked up the pace, and the others danced. Earl told
me decades later that his father had pulled him aside to give
him this simple piece of wedding night advice: "If she doesn't
want to do it, don't do it." Earl's father was a man of few words.
Earl was so embarrassed! Earl said he passed it on to our son,
Sam, when he got married. I laughed.

If you had told me on my wedding day that my future held
years of trouble conceiving and that when God finally gave us a
child, he would take him back to Heaven early, leaving Earl and

me dwelling in a period of sadness so long that we thought we'd died too, if you told me about the horse accident and losing my baby girl, and that one day I'd be sitting here, a widow, smelling my husband's wedding day suit jacket. . . . If you had told me this, I would have run in the other direction. That is why God doesn't reveal the future to us before the future becomes the present. Yes, there's been pain in my life, as there is now, but it's still been a good life. I'm not sorry to have experienced it. Although there have been times when I thought surely He had, God has never given me more than I could handle. And when I open my eyes, I see God's signs of renewed life, like a grandson or the crocus blooming or the summer birds returning.

I sit on a cedar chest at the foot of our bed, holding my husband's jacket and looking out the window for a sign.

∂ANIEL

I figure I'd better let the housemates know what's going on. Rob answers, "Oh, Dan! Thank God it's you! Minda's talking about marrying some bush pilot named Herb and having us be her bridesmaids, but instead of making us wear matching ugly dresses, she wants us to dress up like the Village People, which I, for one, am relieved about, being that my ankles are hideously thick and I always wanted to wear a headdress—dibs on the Indian! However, I have forbidden her to marry any guy named Herb. I'm sure. Herb? 'Ooo, Herb, I love it when you touch me like that!' No, I don't think so. She deserves better, don't you think?"

"Hey, Rob? My grandfather died. I'm going to stay here and help out at least through calving season."

"I'm sorry," Rob says and stops like he doesn't know what to say. "Does this mean you'll be the cowboy in the Village People at Minda's wedding?"

"I thought you weren't going to allow her to marry a guy named Herb" is all I can think to reply.

"Right. Hey, are you coming back? Because if you're not, you know we'll never be able to recruit another housemate with the house like this. If you don't come back, the rest of us will have to clean."

"Don't panic yet. And for God's sake, don't do anything drastic like clean."

EDITH

"Today I need a break from grieving," I tell Mara as she puts another waffle on the iron. I wish it were that easy.

"We could get drunk and bake bread," she suggests.

"No, that would remind me of . . . um"—I lower my head, a little embarrassed—"a special memory of Earl after your oven christening." I smile thinking back to how silly he and I were that late afternoon, and then the pain in my chest hits when I realize I'll never experience anything like that again.

"We could go pick up all your friends at the nursing home and go sing karaoke."

She's trying to make me laugh. I can just imagine Bertha and Madeline making their way to the stage, Bertha with her oxygen tank and Madeline with her walker. Together they sing "Walkin' After Midnight" by Patsy Cline as if either of them could possibly go walking after midnight.

"Well, a change of scenery will probably be necessary to foster a really strong sense of denial," she says.

And that's when it comes to me. "Mara, there used to be a hot spring in the southeast corner of the ranch somewhere. Earl used to take me there when we were newlyweds. I don't know if I'll be able to find it, but I'd like to try. I haven't been on a horseback ride that long in decades, so I might need to turn back."

"That's okay. We'll go on an adventure."

For the last four days the temperatures have been in the forties and fifties. Most of the snow is gone.

Mara has insisted that if we are going to wander around, we need to dress up like gypsies, so we are wearing scarves on our heads and her big, clunky, silver Pakistani jewelry. Her new thoroughbred, Solstice, is decked out in a bareback pad she recovered in velvet and tassels. My horse, Winter, looks much more western, like me from my neck down. Harvey and Zeus are both wearing paisley scarves.

The warm wind blowing up from the south feels comforting. When it hits my face just right, it reminds me of feeling Earl's cheek next to mine when we danced close. I close my eyes and indulge in memories.

When I open them, Mara says, "I love the wind, too. I always think of the Hopi, who believe February winds carry the spirits down from the mountains, back to the village mesas to bring life back, to bring spring."

Funny that we both were thinking of spirits and wind, but in such different ways.

Around noon the winds get stronger and stronger. I see clouds coming in on them, so if we don't want to be drenched in deadly forty-degree rain, we need to turn around now.

Mara gets off her horse, stands with her arms open wide, and completely leans into the wind. She smiles, eyes closed, and shouts, "Edith! You should check this out!" From time to time the wind gusts blow her back a step. Zeus stands next to her, his jaw moving up and down like it does when he hangs his head out the passenger side of her truck.

"I'm afraid if I get off this horse, I'll never be able to get back on again!" Watching the spirits in the wind hold up her whole weight reminds me that it's okay to lean on things I can feel but not see, like God and my Angels. It also reminds me something about the beauty of faith.

"I feel like the wind purifies me!" she shouts over the wind. "Like it sweeps anything that clouds my clarity right off me!"

I think about what she just said and picture the wind blowing the dark cloud off my chest. The heavy numbness of the cloud gives way to the sharp, acute pain of clarity. Pain lets you know that you're alive, I'm told, but then I think if this is what it's going to feel like to be alive without Earl, I don't know if I can bear it. I want so badly to hold him in my arms again, to smell his smell, to hear his voice. I keep picturing the wind sweeping the clouds off me and become aware that I've been crying hard for I don't know how long when Mara stands at my side, rests her head on my thigh, and puts her arm around my hips. My body collapses over her head to rest on Winter's neck as I sob my seemingly endless tears.

DANIEL

"Hey, why don't you ride with me and look for the hot springs your grandmother and I tried to find yesterday?" Mara asks me.

At first I try to think of some reason not to, but then I wonder why I'm doing that. "Sure, okay," I say, and go back to the house to grab my hat and camera.

We saddle up the horses without saying much but a few comments about the weather. She lets Harvey out of his pen. We mount and head off to the southeast, weaving our way through the sagebrush, dog and hog following behind us.

Her horse spooks several times and jumps sideways, throwing Mara off balance. I'm glad she's wearing a helmet. "Your horse seems like a disaster waiting to happen," I say.

"Yeah. He's afraid of places where the grass changes color, white rocks, litter, mud puddles, and stumps, not to mention grouse and deer. Fortunately, Zeus and Harvey seem to flush out most of the wildlife before Solstice gets there. Maybe that's why he seems to feel a little safer when they're out in front. If they ever roam behind a sage bush or something, he just stops and frantically looks for them."

"In fairness to him, the grouse scare me sometimes, too," I say.

"Yeah, they do jump out of nowhere, flapping like crazy. I have this fear that one will get a leg or a wing caught in one of my braids, and I'll have this crazy flapping bird tethered to my head."

I chuckle. It's a funny picture.

We pass some coyote kill, a young deer with its stomach cavity completely eaten out. Mara looks sad.

"During calving season it's war with those guys," I say.

"Dead deer?" she asks, confused.

"Coyotes," I say.

She looks at Zeus. He smells the carcass, runs over, and rolls in it. Then he picks up a leg and runs with it, excitedly.

"He's not sleeping on my bed tonight," she says.

"You let him sleep on your bed?"

"It's like being tucked in all night—tightly sealed, no drafts. Keeps me warm."

"Wait until tick season. The first time you find a tick in your bed, you'll change your mind real fast."

"Ew," she says.

From the bluff we ended up on, we can see steam from a

gulch below. We skirt the edge and look for the easiest way down.

"This looks like a fabulous place for a wreck," she says and dismounts. She clips a lead rope to Solstice's halter and slips the bridle off his head. "If he freaks out and I have to let go, you'll give me a ride back, right?" she only half-jokes.

"It'll cost you," I say.

As we get closer, I catch a whiff of that rotten-egg sulfur smell and dismount. "Water your horse?" I offer. She hands me the rope. I walk to the stream with the horses, followed by the dog and hog, while she investigates the springs.

"Hey, this is the one!" she calls to me. "You going in?"

I shrug and listen to the sweet sound of horses slurping.

The next time I look over, she's already in; there's a pile of clothes on the ground next to her. I tie the horses and walk over. "How's the water?" I ask.

"Heavenly. You're missing out."

I'm missing out. Yes, I'm definitely missing out. I'm missing out in so many ways. She doesn't even have a clue how right she is. Neither of us says anything for the longest time.

"Hey, you doin' okay?" She opens her eyes to watch my answer.

I don't know what to say, so I give her a look to ask why she asked that.

"I don't know. Sometimes you just seem very far away. Sometimes you even seem invisible."

I don't know what to say to that, either, but I look down and nod a little to let her know I know what she's talking about. I look at the water and wonder what my problem is. I take off my clothes and get in.

What we don't notice while down in the heavenly gulch is that the winds shift and pick up, bringing with them heavy clouds from the southwest. By the time we see them, they are overhead.

We dry off and dress as quickly as we can. She puts on a raincoat. I look at her, surprised she brought rain gear. We mount up and take off at a fast trot, scanning the ground in front of us for any coyote dens or other holes. The clouds above thicken up and begin to drop rain. By the time we arrive home, we're cold and drenched.

"Sauna?" she proposes through blue lips.

"Sounds good," I say.

❧

A cloud of steam rises up from where she threw water on the stove. "Smart to always carry rain gear," I say.

"You know, you'd think after all the times I've been caught in rain or hail out of nowhere, I would, but I usually don't. I had a dream last night where my Gram and I were riding camels across the Sahara, and she told me to bring it today. When I looked at the sky this morning, I figured maybe her wires were crossed. But then I figured she didn't specify I'd need it for rain, so I brought it anyway."

I can't tell if she's making this up or if she's serious.

"Do your parents ever come to you in dreams?" she asks.

I shake my head and wonder where she's going with this, but she doesn't say anything more. "I had a dream about you once, before I met you—right before I came back," I confess.

"Well, yeah. I tried calling you on the telephone, but you never answered," she says.

"Wait, so you're telling me you chose to be in my dream, and then you just did it?" I ask, disturbed.

"If I'm worried about something, I tend to go there when I'm sleeping, you know, to try to fix it," she explains.

"What do you mean 'go there'?"

"I guess it's sort of like being a ghost. Your spirit leaves your body, and you go wherever you want without paying plane fare."

"So you, what? Jumped into my head?" I ask, a little angry.

"No way," she assures me. "I would never jump in someone's body. Ew. That's worse than borrowing their underwear."

"So how did you get in *my* dream?"

"That dimension doesn't just belong to you, Daniel. It belongs to everybody. Okay, so I did let myself into your house, but I knew something was wrong with your grandfather and that he had unfinished business with you."

"How'd you know that?" I ask.

"Know what?"

"That something was wrong with him," I say.

"Clouds," she says. "He had clouds around his neck."

"Clouds?"

"Yeah, clouds. Or smoke. Cloudy like that."

"Do I have clouds around me?" I ask nervously.

"No, you have almost nothing around you," she answers.

"Is that good?"

"Not really. It's like you're stuck or stagnant. No movement. Shut down."

What do you say to that? "Oh," I say.

"Try dancing around your house," she advises.

For a long time we just breathe in the hot air and let it warm our bones, but then I get to thinking about Grandpa's spirit and wondering where he was exactly.

"Do you believe in Heaven?" I ask Mara.

"Yes," she says. "I've been there."

"You died?" I ask.

"No, just visited, like I visited you," she says.

"You dreamt you were in Heaven," I clarify.

"I didn't stay long enough to find out if there were dogs there. I really want to know where the dogs were. I can't imagine Heaven without dogs."

Then neither of us says anything else. We just breathe in the steam, shut our eyes, and lose ourselves in our own thoughts.

EDITH

Mara and I sit back, naked in the hot springs a week after our first attempt to find them. I go inside myself, as one would go inside a house that had been struck by a tornado, to survey the damage, see what is left, and try to straighten up what remains.

Eventually, she breaks the silence. I open one eye when she begins to talk.

"You know, Edith, I accept that I'll never find a man who can handle all this woman." She gestures at her whole body in an upward motion with her hands and kind of laughs. "But I do struggle with the decision to have kids."

"Hm," I reply, shutting my eyes. My soul feels too tired to struggle with something I already struggled with decades ago. Of course, in my day it wasn't really a choice. It was just something you did. But there are struggles associated with fulfilling expectations, too.

"I went through a time a year ago when I was feeling intense grief, mostly on a biological level, about not having a child. I was even asking a couple of my platonic male friends with really nice genetics if they would donate sperm to my worthy cause. Lately, though, I look at all it takes, and it scares me. I like my life, Edith. I like bathing when I want, sleeping in, having stained-glass shards all over my house, and riding spirited horses."

"Hm," I reply again.

"Would you do it again, Edith?"

I take a deep breath. Would I do it again? "You know, Mara, when Sam died, I thought I would die, too. It felt like the life just drained out of me, out of my core. Losing a child is the worst thing that can happen to anyone. For a while, I confess, I did think motherhood was a cruel form of torture. You pour your heart, your soul, your life into this child, and eventually this child, who has no idea what a huge piece of you they are, goes recklessly out into this world, and all you can do is watch, hope, pray, and have faith. In an instant the most important accomplishment of your life can be destroyed." I open my eyes. "I looked at all this. And yet when it came down to it, by being a mother I learned a whole new level of love. I'm not sorry to have experienced that. I'm not sorry to have experienced rocking my baby to sleep in my arms." I pause to squint the hot tears out of the corners of my eyes. "In fact, I can't imagine my life without having had that." And I shut my eyes again.

For a long time neither of us says anything. Finally, Mara says, "I think being a mother is the bravest thing any woman can do."

We sit back together, arms floating, eyes closed, and I look forward to seeing my baby in Heaven. I wonder if he and Earl are watching me now. Hm. I wonder if I should be wearing a swimsuit. I smile to myself.

MARA

Have you ever woken up in the middle of the night to see a hologram of a face floating above, looking down at you? I've personally not had this experience before, but I figure, hey, if a face shows up, it's probably best to be polite. So I ask, "May I help you?"

She speaks to me with her thoughts. I just sort of hear her in my head. She tells me that Wade, a student in my fifth-period class, is questioning whether he has the strength to live another day.

"What can I do?" I ask.

She tells me to speak to the whole class about what depression is and to tell them to take care of each other. When I ask if he will be okay, she tells me that his serotonin level will come back up on its own without antidepressants and just to reassure him.

I say, "Okay," and with that she floats up, up, and out of the corner of my room.

Now the task is figuring out how to do my true work. I mean, I can't really walk into class and tell them I have a message from Wade's Guardian, now, can I?

DANIEL

I had almost forgotten about Three Hills and Saint Patrick's Day. Being that pretty much everyone in town is Irish, it's big—so big, in fact, that the Saint Pat's decorations begin to displace Valentine's Day stuff in Murray's Drug Store sometime around February 5. I duck into Murray's to pick up three plaid hats with furry fake red hair attached to them to send to the housemates. I watch the parade from the curb with Grandma and Mara. The kids parade by and shout at her.

The Girl Scouts hold a long Girl Scout banner as they walk side by side. "Hi, Ms. O'Shaunnessey!" they call to her, and she yells hello back. A truckload of Cub Scouts in their uniforms drive by and wave enthusiastically at her. She smiles and waves back, just as happy to see them. Then comes a truckload of fifth- and sixth-grade football players who are trying not to look as excited as they are but attempting to look cool instead, but anyone can tell they're about to burst with pride. She waves at them, too. The junior high band notices her applauding out of the corner of their eyes.

This is my home, but you'd never know it. No one looks at me to see if I'm watching them play the flute.

"Aren't they all so precious?" she asks us, not really expecting an answer. "Those are my babies!" she proudly declares.

As the parade ends, Tim walks by, stops, and shouts, "Hey!"

"Hey!" I shout back.

"Hello, Mrs. McRae, Mara," he says politely.

"Hello, Timothy," Grandma replies. I think she called him Timothy just to bug him.

"How's the hog?" he asks Mara.

"Great," she answers.

"On your way to the Elks, Tim?" I ask.

"Of course," he answers with a shit-eatin' grin but then turns to Grandma and solemnly says, "It's all about helping children, ma'am."

Knowingly, Grandma says, "Uh-huh."

"Yeah, we're putting on a mutton stew dinner. Five bucks a bowl. Comes with corn bread. Proceeds go to children's charities. Hope you can make it. I'd love to stay, but I said I'd help cook."

I point to a nearby fire truck. "I see the Elks have already made preparations for your cooking debut."

"Yeah, you know, an ounce of prevention . . . ," he says, playing along. Grandma forces a smile and gives a courtesy laugh.

"Ladies, it's been a pleasure." Tim tips his hat at them and rushes off.

Grandma turns to Mara and says, "Stay away from that one."

A short redheaded teenager starts to pass us. She has a black eye, and I think she might be pregnant. She looks up at Mara.

"Hey, Kelli, how's it going? Enjoy the parade?" Mara asks her.

The girl shrugs, smiles, and keeps walking.

"Excuse me," Mara says to us and jogs down the sidewalk after the girl. She catches up and talks to her quietly for a minute. Mara gestures to her own eye. The girl shakes her head and shrugs. Mara looks concerned and touches the girl on her arm for a second before returning to us.

"Everything okay?" Grandma asks.

"I doubt it, but my hands are tied," Mara answers. "Sometimes all you can do is love them the best you can and hope it's enough."

"Hm," Grandma says, nodding in agreement.

"Sometimes I think I make a difference, and other times I feel so very small compared to all the suffering in the world. There are moments I don't think I make any difference at all. When it's all said and done, though, of course I have. Of course we all make a difference. How could the world not be a different place in the places we have walked, right?" She seems like she's trying to convince herself.

"Of course," Grandma says.

The street appears to be in anarchy with the fallout from the parade—clowns, Shriners on minibikes, little kids looking for their parents, and a couple of giant leprechauns.

"How about we go watch the sheepdog trials?" Grandma proposes.

"You guys go ahead," Mara says. "I'm thinkin' I'm going to harvest some good vegetarian karma at the ewe doo bingo. Since I've never eaten lamb, I'm thinkin' that little lamb can surely dookie in my square and make me a hundred dollars richer as a way of saying thanks."

She gives us a look soliciting agreement, but we just chuckle at her a little. "How 'bout I hook up with you guys at the O'Team roping later?"

"Sure," Grandma and I say, and get in the car to go out to the Doherty ranch to watch the sheepdogs. On our way out, Grandma gestures at a cow, her head over the fence, watching the cars go by.

"You ever feel like that?" she asks.

"Like a cow?" I ask back.

"Like that cow," she answers, "just sitting there, watching the world go by?"

I don't know what to say. "Owen and Bertha entering a dog this year?" I say, changing the subject.

"No," she says with resignation, the sadness at her failed effort to reach out to me coming through in the tone of her voice.

"What about Hank? He going to enter that little Fifi dog of his?" Surely that will make her laugh.

"Don't reckon so," she answers with the same sadness. I can't stand it. I can't stand making Grandma sadder.

I wait a couple minutes and then, finally, I just blurt out: "Look, Grandma. What is it that you want from me?"

"I want you to wake up, Daniel." And when I don't respond to that, she adds, "It's like you're just sleepwalking all the time. Sometimes I just want to give you a good shake. For God's sake, wake up."

"I'm trying, Grandma," I whisper.

She nods, and I turn off the highway to the sheepdog trials.

OARA

School is going well, I guess. I gave my depression speeches—and tackled child abuse and drug abuse while I was at it. Wade is making friends and seems to be happier. The school counselor told me he moved here with his dad because his parents are getting a divorce. That's a lot of changes.

Rumor has it that a student of mine is pregnant, and by the way the staff whispered about it in the staff room, you would've thought someone was dying. I wonder when motherhood became such a failure. I don't really understand. While I like my job, I've never really found it to be the all-encompassing embodiment of fulfillment like I thought it would be. Motherhood strikes me as a much more meaningful way to spend your life. In my mind I say a silent blessing for the student.

OANIEL

I go out and check on the two-year-old heifers. They've begun to calve. I see one calf who isn't nursing. One of the quarters of the mother's bag is smaller than the others, and when that's the case, it's easy to think he has drunk. Not all quarters of a heifer's bag are always even, though. The calf has a big hump in his back. He's hungry. I get him up and get him nursed.

I can see the water bag on another heifer. I need to check on her in another hour and a half or so. If she doesn't get that calf out in two hours or less, there's a problem.

I ride out to check on the three-year-olds. Mamas and babies are looking good. I see a heifer on the ground with the calf's front feet coming out of the birth canal. I wait long enough to see the calf's head making it out, right over the feet. They're fine. I ride on.

Coyotes have been out with the older cows. I see one dead calf with hoofprints all around it. Dammit. When two or more coyotes team up on a cow and calf, the cow keeps the coyotes at bay but tramples her own calf in the process. I should have brought a gun with me.

I see another humped-up calf. His mother has big tits, and he is having trouble getting them into his mouth. I stay and help.

❧

I photograph my room, the toys that are still in my closet, and the red model airplane still hanging from the ceiling. I lie on my bed and photograph the ceiling I stared at so many times. I photograph the photographs of my parents that hang on the wall in the hall that I pass on my way to the bathroom. I photograph the photographs of me bull riding.

I study one closely, the one where I'm on the ground and the bull's feet land inches from my neck. For the first time I see how bull riding was my way of playing Russian roulette. I see my complete ambivalence about living, both in the past and recently. And I ponder the irony of how bull riding was seen as such a brave thing when, in fact, it was a completely chicken shit thing for me to do, something I did because I was too afraid to pull the trigger myself and definitely too afraid to commit to life. I take the bull-riding pictures off the wall and set them facedown on the dresser. I don't want to be that boy on the bull anymore.

I go downstairs and photograph Grandma on the front porch looking up to the sky, like she does so often, and then out to the horizon, almost as if she is resigning herself to staying here on Earth when she would rather be above.

ᴍᴀʀᴀ

I was watching some documentary about Monet. One line of the whole movie resonated for me: "It is said Monet did not want to merely paint objects; he wanted to paint the air around his objects." So I can't help but wonder if Monet had been one of us. He is, after all, known as "The Master of Light."

Presently, I'm building a giant sun sculpture for my purple garden. I've collected numerous yellow, white, and clear glass candy dishes and drinking glasses. I drilled holes through all of them and am now attempting to hook them all with copper wire to a frame I welded together that hangs from a tree. Then I'll add some more . . . something—I'm not sure what—to suggest radiance. So far it's not working, but I'm not giving up on fifty dollars' worth of thrift store crap that easily.

One thing about teaching that is really challenging to me is that I truly believe art class in itself is a contradiction, and yet sometimes I find myself thinking rather strong critical thoughts about students' work. I don't want to have these thoughts about their work. Really, I just want to encourage them to experiment and to love art.

So when I find myself thinking critical thoughts, I know it's time to turn my focus back on my own work. It's working. This stupid project is humbling.

I've been thinking about Lady Godiva and how all she was trying to do was bless the farmers' fields with good fertility blessings, and how she was misunderstood. Just because she didn't feel like wearing clothes, her sacred ride was manipulated into something perverse. I'm going to do some kind of Lady

Godiva monument in my garden. She can bless my garden, and I won't twist her intention.

I wonder, if Monet were alive, how he'd paint the light around Lady Godiva, how he'd show that the blessings radiating from her hands were real. Blessings are such a powerful energy, like wind in a way; you can see neither, but both affect the physical world. This will be my next challenge.

EDITH

Roses have sprung up around my porch. All kinds. The climbing ones are everywhere. I know this is the work of Earl.

When Daniel rides out to check on calves or goes into town, I put on "The Tennessee Waltz," open the windows so I can hear it outside, come out here on the porch, and waltz. Maybe I'm waltzing by myself. Maybe not. I like to think Earl is with me. I wear rose oil and put roses in my hair to entice him.

DANIEL

I walk through the fairgrounds at night, lost. Lights blink everywhere, on all the rides and in all the booths. Happy people eat corn dogs and win prizes at game booths. Couples walk hand in hand. All the little kids carry giant stuffed animals.

"Mom? Dad?" I call out. "Mom? Dad?"

Mara crosses my path, riding the white horse with the feathers tied in its mane again. She holds some cotton candy. Some of it is stuck to her face.

"Mara? What are you doing here?" I ask.

"What do you mean?" she asks back.

"This is my recurring dream where I can't find my parents," I explain.

"Do you know where you are?" she asks.

Just then I hear my grandparents call out to us from their seat on the Ferris wheel. They wave enthusiastically and look younger. "Yoo-hoo! Daniel! Mara!"

"Hello!" Mara calls back.

Their bench reaches the top of the Ferris wheel, and they kiss.

"She sure missed him," Mara says.

We watch the Ferris wheel descend down the back side. As it nears, Mara calls out to Edith: "So, Edith, just visiting, I hope?"

"That was the plan, but I want to stay!" Grandma answers.

"Do you know where you are yet?" Mara asks me.

My eyes fly open, and I gasp as I bolt upright. It's morning. I look at my door with dread. I get out of bed and nervously walk to my grandparents' door. Outside I tap gently with one knuckle.

"Grandma?" I call quietly. No answer. I open the door and slowly approach. She lies on her back. The morning light filters through her sheer blue curtains, casting an eerie light on her. "Grandma?"

I reach for her hand. It's cold. I jerk back reflexively.

I hear Mara storm through the back door, up the stairs, and into the room. "Oh," she says and begins to cry. "She stayed."

Mara embraces me from behind and sort of rocks. I just stand and stare at Grandma, stunned and numb.

SPRING

DANIEL

I never understood those people who blew their brains out indoors so that someone else had to scrub their remains off the walls and such. I don't know if suicide is immoral, but I know making someone else clean up after it is. So I take Grandpa's gun out from under his bed and walk through the two-year-old heifers out to the east hay field. I find myself walking toward the old Russian olive tree Grandpa used to marvel over. He couldn't figure out how it lived in such dry soil so far away from a spring or a creek. As a boy I would think if that tree could survive here, I probably could, too, but now . . . now I'm tired of being left behind. And I'm tired of the isolated life I've created for myself. I sit near the tree and watch it for a while. The way the branches sway sort of soothes me . . . hypnotic somehow.

This decision is so permanent, and I start to wonder if maybe everyone thinks about doing this at some point. I remember when I was seven, I mucked up a model train I was working on. I thought it was wrecked and had every intention of smashing it into little pieces, but Dad caught my arm midair and told me to give it twenty-four hours before I smashed it. Said sometimes things look different the next day. Sure enough, the next day it seemed clear to me how to go about fixing it, and I was cooled off enough to follow through.

I think of my dad and decide to give it a night. I pull two calves on my way home.

It's another frosty morning with new snow just a couple hundred feet higher in elevation than the house. I drink my coffee inside while the truck warms up, in hopes of avoiding scraping the windshield, which I hate doing. Then I drive to the hay barn, load up the truck, and drive up into the hills until I find cattle to feed. I hate the stillness of the morning, and I hate waking up when it's dark.

The morning is clear, and light shades of pink and violet reveal themselves as the sun approaches the horizon. The truck bumps along the field.

Finally I spot the heifers and several calves. I dump bale after bale out of the truck. Steam and smells from the cattle fill the still air.

When I try to leave, I discover that I'm stuck because the weight over my rear wheels is gone. "Shit!" I start yelling, and it feels good. "Shit! Shit!" I yell as I dig out the tires. As I scoop the snow with my hands, I'm overwhelmed by the urge to throw snowballs at the cattle. "Why are you so stupid?" I yell and fire off a snowball. I fire off more snowballs, yelling "Stupid!" each time I throw one, although I know in reality it's not the cattle I'm so mad at. I'm mad about being left behind.

Soon words don't seem angry enough for me, so I just start making angry noises while I fire off more and more snowballs with less and less accuracy. The cattle stay a little ways back but keep glancing longingly at the hay. Now snowballs are not satisfying enough for the anger in my arms, so I start pushing the truck in thrusts while yelling my grunts. Eventually, the truck starts moving, but I'm not done, so I keep pushing the truck, running behind it, occasionally slipping in the snow and once hitting my chin on the tailgate. But I don't care. I don't care about anything. I don't care which direction I'm going, and I don't care if this truck rolls down a hill and smashes into bits.

I've been pushing and running for probably a half mile when my neighbor, Owen, drives up on his four-wheeler. "Son! Son!" he calls to me. "Want me to get the tractor and pull that in for you? What's the problem? Transmission?"

I stop and look at him, feeling sort of defeated, exposed, and a little embarrassed. I don't know what to say or how to explain this.

"Well?" Owen's voice booms out of his barrel chest. I just sort of stand there, shoulders rolled in, mouth open, and nothing coming out of my mouth.

"Son, are you okay?"

I'm not sure how to answer that. I suspect, though, that in this world where ninety-eight percent of all problems are solved by someone telling you to "cowboy up," I better just answer yes. "Yes, sir."

"What's the problem with your truck?"

"Actually, sir, there's no problem. It'll get me back just fine."

"Well, then, why in God's name are you pushing it, son?" It's weird to have him call me *son*. It hits a trigger with me, but then another part of me finds it sort of comforting.

"I was just blowing off steam."

He looks at me carefully. "You meltin' down on us, son?"

"Nah," I say, looking down at the ground, shaking my head slightly, and smiling enough to convince him I'm all right, which I guess I am.

"Okay, then."

I take that as my cue to hop in the cab and go. And at that point any anger I had turns back into that familiar lonely numbness.

❧

I stare at the sky behind the branches for a while—white billowy clouds passing across the blue—and wonder what it will be like

149

to float through that sky or become part of it or whatever happens, assuming I don't go straight to hell. I can't believe I would go to hell for this. Surely God has compassion and mercy.

The tree sways back and forth the way my mother used to rock me. I remember I went through this time where I was afraid to go to sleep. She wouldn't make me go back to bed, where for some reason I felt so afraid. She'd make me some Campbell's vegetable beef soup or sometimes split pea with bacon and then let me fall asleep on her lap while she stroked my hair. I shut my eyes and let myself go back there, to the comfort of her lap, listening to her hum a lullaby, and the rhythmic combing of my bangs.

When I open my eyes, Mara sits next to me, while Zeus is off sniffing holes in the ground. "Beautiful tree," she says.

"Yup," I don't look at her. I keep my eyes on the branches. Then we sit there for at least a half hour in silence.

"What's the gun for?" she asks.

"Coyotes," I half-lie.

I can tell she's not sure whether to believe my story. Then she says gently, "Come on, friend. Let's go back and eat some soup."

❧

I am looking at the tree from the back porch today when Whitey comes ripping up the driveway. He stops abruptly, gets out, and strides over.

"Come on, boy," he says firmly. "You've got a ranch to run. You got a thousand pregnant cows calving." I guess I move too slow, because he adds, "Don't just sit there like a sack of shit, boy. Get up." Whitey never swears.

He waits in the doorway while I step in to grab my hat, and he notices the gun where I left it on a bench near the door. "Give me your piece, boy," he says firmly. I hand him the pistol.

He takes the bullets out and puts them in his pocket, muttering, "If you got a coyote problem, you're gonna have to call me because your gun privileges have just been revoked." That's when I realize Mara sent him.

We don't talk much today. We pull two calves. Then we find a set of twins. I put one of the twins on my saddle in front of me to put on one of the nurse cows in the barn. Keeping track of one calf in a big herd is about all a cow can manage on a good day. Keeping track of two is impossible. If the twins aren't split up, at least one will get lost and starve to death.

When the sun goes down, Whitey invites himself in for some of Mrs. Farley's chicken casserole. "I'll be out tomorrow to help you replace that rotted H brace near your gate," he says.

"You don't need to do that," I reply.

He just looks at me as if to ask if I'm challenging him. "Be ready at two-thirty" is all he says, and with that he takes his dishes to the sink and leaves.

❧

I sit in the front pew alone.

Whitey and Mara sit behind me, on the aisle. On the other side of the aisle sit the Grennans. Hank and his family sit behind them.

"To everything there is a season and a time and purpose under Heaven," Father McCleary says.

"Are you okay?" Mara whispers to me.

I whisper back, "Yeah."

Father McCleary stands next to Edith's casket in his long robe. I sit and ponder those who truly believe God likes them better than others. "We don't know where Edith is now, so we must pray for her soul," he says. Rage boils inside me. I want to punch him. I want to punch him right in his pompous face.

How dare he! She was a good woman. They don't come any better. So how dare he call her character into question. How dare he call her spirit into question. It would feel so good to punch him. It would feel so good to stand and yell, "I know where she is! Anyone who knew her knows where she is!" I want to stand and defend her, but I know that if she were here, that would not be what she'd want. She would not want her service turned into a three-ring circus.

"I know where she is," I whisper to no one.

"She's at the fair," Mara whispers back.

I chuckle. That's right. She's at the fair.. And I'm so glad I'm not the only one who knows. I'm so glad I'm not the only one who knows the truth. I know that my grandmother's soul was never in any danger and that she's just fine. And it doesn't matter if people give all kinds of money to the church today, because no one needs to buy her way into Heaven. She's fine.

Then Father McCleary says, "We will all end up here. We never know when it will be our time. We must always be absolved of our sins and be in a state of grace." After today I am never, ever setting foot in here again. Not for anyone.

MARA

For me gardening is a form of prayer. Most people have an awareness of life and death, but few have an awareness of life, death, and life again. Gardeners do, though.

Bulbs come up every spring. Then in winter it looks like there's nothing there, no hope for life ever again. Then, hallelujah! Next spring they're back even fuller. It's the same thing with perennials.

Annuals have a slightly different lesson, though. Annuals

really do die, but they broadcast seeds before they go. Where there was only one calendula the year before, there will be ten this year, and one day they will fill every empty space in the garden. Annuals are a lesson in the difference that one living thing—plant or person—can make and how its presence resonates long after it's gone. There again, the effects are not immediate. There is always the winter.

And when you consider the garden as a whole, well, winter is a time to reflect, a time to dream. It gives you time to ask the big questions, like: Is there any reason my vegetable garden design should be boring simply because it's utilitarian? Then when spring comes, maybe you plant your vegetables in a design that looks like a Celtic knot instead of sensible, uninspired rows.

Gardening is an affirmation of divine timing. Some years in early spring my enthusiasm takes an ugly turn, and I seemingly believe I can make spring happen earlier than it normally would if I just work hard enough, if I till enough, compost enough, and harden off seedlings earlier than I normally would. In the end I wind up with twelve flats of dead seedlings. Then I direct-seed a couple months later, and with much less effort everything grows into the full glory it was destined to encompass. To everything there is a season. Amen.

After Edith's funeral today, I really need all these prayers. I put my hands in the earth where for me the truth resides. Zeus lies on the ground next to me and then gets up and runs over to Daniel. Daniel pets Zeus and walks over.

"Hey, you okay?" I ask.

He looks off and shakes his head. It's a small gesture, but I can see his anger.

"That service was brutal," I say.

He looks at the ground and nods with the same anger.

"Being around so many people with such different perceptions and beliefs about death—I mean ascension—can really mess me up," I say.

"The last thing I needed to listen to were insults directed at her," he says.

"Yeah, no shit. I mean, I think services must have originally been invented to comfort the people closest to the person who passed. Personally, that didn't comfort me. I can see it didn't comfort you, either," I say.

"No," he says bitterly.

"But this was a tricky one because we both know that while Edith was on Earth, she thought the priest's words had magic powers. While she was living, knowing she was going to have that service meant something to her. Now that she's at the fair, she's probably changed her mind. But, still, those were her wishes when she was living, and you had to go on that," I say. "You were in a tough spot."

"That's the last time," he says. "That's the last time I ever go there. I'm not sitting through one more funeral."

"Yeah, I always marvel at how friends and family from many churches and faiths are asked or expected to come to a funeral, and yet the hosting church never shows any respect for the sacred beliefs or deeply held convictions of others. Ministers and priests always seem to see it as open season, a time to impose their beliefs on the vulnerable, a time for a come-to-Jesus infomercial. It disgusts me," I say.

"Exactly," he says.

"That's why I'm gardening now. When I touch the dirt, I imagine the energy of my anger being absorbed by the earth where it can be transformed into something useful, something good. The earth is all about turning waste into nutrients. Want to join?"

He squats next to me and pulls a button weed. Zeus leans up against him.

"Weeding is therapeutic on so many levels," I say. "I often see it as an exercise in getting rid of invasive, non-native thought patterns in the garden of my soul—you know, pulling up things that are taking over, things that aren't working, making room for what I desire. It's an exercise in the power of intention. I intend to grow sweet peas. So I do. First, though, I make room for them. So as I weed, I think about all the things in my life I intend to manifest and all the things I need to weed out to make room. Usually boils down to weeding out fear to make room for love."

He laughs at me as he pulls a knapweed and a dandelion. "Nothing is simple for you, is it? I mean, weeding isn't just weeding, and dreams aren't just dreams, and dogs aren't just dogs."

I laugh at myself. "I don't know. It all seems so obvious to me. Is obvious the same thing as simple?"

"No," he says with a smile. Then Whitey drives up, and Daniel leaves me to weed by myself and consider how clarity and simplicity may or may not be similar.

DANIEL

Whitey and I pull the rotted H braces and replace the posts with new timbers.

"Listen close, now," he begins. "I'm going to tell you the secret to life." He takes a moment to peer out of his deeply hooded eyes at me. "Fences are like a person's life. Sometimes it's up and strong, and all these posts are all the things that keep the life up and strong: a loving spouse and family, health, work, neighbors. You get the idea. Sometimes even dreams make good fence posts.

"Your problem," he continues, "is that you ain't got enough fence posts to hold up your life. And many of the ones that you do got are rotted. You got to get you some fence posts, boy. And if you got a neighbor who wants to help you put them in, by God, you let him. One day he might need help with his own fence, and if he helped you, it'll be easier for him to ask for your help. You get it?"

I nod as I begin to think about what he just said. I picture my life as a fence—long strings of barbed wire drooping and sagging between the rare and rotted fence posts. And I have no idea how to get me some more fence posts.

❧

"Paul?"

"Dan. My friend. We have some killer raccoons residing on our back patio now. They wield camping utensils they stole from the garage. I thought maybe if I put some home brew out there, they would get drunk and pass out, and I could return to my favorite chair out there. But they just got drunk enough to be angered by their own reflection in the sliding glass door. They crashed into it all night with forks in their hands. It was really scary, Dan. And I think they ate Lavern."

"Aw, no. Hey, Paul, I'm sorry to hear that."

"Rob can't even scare them away by singing the Bee Gees anymore."

"Well, my friend, I think you're going to have to break down and pay the garbage bill."

"Shush!"

"Hey, listen, Paul. My grandma died now."

"Oh, man. I'm really sorry."

"I haven't figured out what I'm going to do just yet, but rent is in the mail."

"Thanks, man, because I go out on the boat in less than two

months, so if you move out, you all will have to clean without me."

"You're too kind, Paul."

"Hey, do you need us down there? Because I'm free for six weeks, Rob's not on the boat yet, and Minda tore something in her knee, so she's off for the summer."

I start to say no, that I don't need help, but before the words make it out my mouth, I realize I do. "Yeah, I could use help down here," I say.

"We'll fly out tomorrow if we can," he says, and immediately I feel like something has been lifted off me.

"I'm happy to help out with tickets," I say.

"Minda could probably use help in light of her injury, and Rob might, too. No worries, my friend. Between you and me and our big fish dollars, we'll make sure everyone's covered. You and I can figure it out later. Oh, hey, Minda's coming. I have to go out there and distract the 'coons so she can make it to the house. Okay?"

"Thanks, man. And bring your rubber boots."

❧

When I answer the back door, Mara simply says, "I still don't know how to two-step," as if teaching a dance lesson is exactly what I want to do the night after my grandmother's service. I take a good long look at her and think.

"I haven't slept in days, I've got more calving to do, and I've got to make room for houseguests by tomorrow night," I say.

She doesn't budge. "I'll help you calve and clean your house."

I take a deep breath, too tired to fight with her. "Come on in," I finally say. I walk to the living room, pull an old Patsy Cline LP out of its sleeve, and play "Walkin' After Midnight." It's slow. I push the coffee table up to the couch to make room.

Mara waits. "Quick-quick, slow . . . slow. Quick-quick, slow . . . slow. Quick-quick, slow . . . slow," I count off first. "Ready?" I ask, holding my arms out in the dancing position.

"Wait. That's only three beats of dancing to music that has four beats per measure. That doesn't make sense," she says.

"No, it doesn't," I agree.

"Are you sure you've got it right? Are you sure it's not really a type of waltz?"

"Look, Mara, it was invented by white people. It doesn't make sense. Do you want to learn it or not?"

"I want to learn it."

"Quick-quick, slow . . . slow. Back on your right. Ready?" I lead and she follows. She catches on quickly as we dance around the room. She watches our feet.

I try to remember when the last time was that I danced with a woman. It's been a long, long time. Then for the first time, I really notice how beautiful Mara is. She looks up at me, smiling, and I snap out of it. I mean, that could never work. And, anyway, I want to sell the ranch and return to Alaska. Plus, even if we did get together, one day she'd leave. "You've got it," I say. "That's it. Now you know how to two-step." I stop dancing.

"That's it?"

"That's it." We stand awkwardly facing each other for a moment.

"Well, okay. Thanks for the lesson," she says, like she's sorry it's over.

I've got to tell her what I decided. "Wait, Mara." I search for a way to begin. "I'm thinking about selling the ranch."

She looks surprised and concerned.

"It's just that, you know, this was never really a happy place for me," I explain. "Or maybe you don't know. My grandparents weren't always the people you knew. Throughout my whole childhood they hardly talked at all. After my parents died, everyone was just so sad."

"Yeah."

"And, you know, I'm more of a fisherman than a rancher."

"I understand."

"I know you and my grandfather had some kind of agreement about you living here." She looks at the floor. "It's just . . . I don't know if I could live my life here. I don't know if I could stand it."

She keeps her head down and walks toward the back door. She puts her hand on the doorknob. "Selling is a big and irreversible decision. If I were you, I'd take my time with that one."

"I've got to decide in a month. If I want to make salmon season, I can't have cattle."

"You don't have to decide tonight."

"I suppose I don't."

"Tonight is a bad decision-making night," she says.

"That could be," I agree.

"Good night," she says.

"Good night," I say back. "Hey, Mara? I don't know if you were the reason my grandparents were happy again there for a while, but if you were, thank you."

"I'm just a few steps away if you need me." She walks out the door back toward her place. I shut the door gently behind her.

Downstairs I dust the master bedroom my grandparents never used. They liked the view from their upstairs room, they claimed, but I suspect they moved up there for me—so I wouldn't be all alone and scared up there after my parents died. The downstairs bedroom is ready for a guest.

Upstairs is harder. Mara cleaned my grandparents' bedroom after Grandma died, but I feel funny having anyone stay in it. I don't want anyone to move anything. Minda would just get that. I'll put her in there.

Finally, there is the room that used to be my dad's when he was a kid. I went upstairs to the door with the ceramic sign on it that read SAM. I opened the door we never opened and turned on the light.

My father's train track snakes all around the room. His Tonto bow and arrow hangs on the wall. If I put Rob in here, he would play with them. I'll put Paul in here. A few rodeo trophies of his sit on his dresser, two for saddle broncs, one for bareback, and one for bull riding. A handful of 4-H ribbons hang from the corner of the mirror. It wasn't unlike the way my room had been, except he also had some pictures of my mother tucked into the frame of his mirror. I never had that. I never had someone I wanted to marry. I never even had a serious relationship—drunken lovers, sure, a few, but anything significant, no.

The bedding is dusty. I pull sheets and blankets out of their neatly tucked corners. Stripping the blankets off my father's bed seems sacrilegious. I just destroyed part of the Sam museum. Instead of feeling bad, though, a good feeling washes over me. I feel like maybe he's watching me and trying to tell me that making room for the present is a good thing and that he knows I don't need a museum bedroom to remember him. I feel like he's applauding my choice to begin to make room for a living family. "Thanks, Dad," I say. Then I carry the wad of bedding down to the creepy basement and stick half of it in the washing machine. Once I start the machine, I run out of the basement and up the stairs.

❦

It's two-thirty a.m., and like the three previous nights, I can't sleep in this house. I go to my room to change my clothes, and that's it. I leave my window wide open so I don't have to mess with it when my lungs freeze up. There will never be enough air in there. If I sleep at all, it's with my head on the dining room table. The kitchen is the only room in this house that I can breathe in.

From my place at the dining room table I can look across the backyard and see Mara's light still on. She stays up late on weekends. From time to time I can see her silhouette cross through the stained-glass window, sometimes carrying something, sometimes dancing alone, sometimes dancing with Zeus.

I put my coat on and walk out to survey the two-year-old heifers. Not much going on. No problems. Satisfied, I begin to walk back, passing Mara's house. I turn and pause. Light streams out into the dark night from her stained-glass windows and reflects on the frost that coats the ground. I go up to her door and knock.

"Hello, friend," she says as she opens her door wide and shuts it behind me. "Welcome to the Church of the Dog." I follow her past all her paintings in progress all over the walls: in her image . . . some Angels, some mermaids, some with Zeus and horses.

She pours me some tea from a kettle of water on the wood-stove. "You can't sleep there, can you?"

I just shake my head.

We sit on the little futon she uses for a couch near the fire, and she rubs my back while I sip tea.

"My life is such a mess," I blurt out.

"Lots of weeds?"

"And nothing I grew on purpose," I add. "My family is all gone," I choke out and turn my head so she can't see the tears that stream down my face.

She puts her arm around my back and rests her head on my shoulder. "I'll be your family," she softly offers.

I put down the teacup and swing my legs up in one motion, resting my head in her lap, lying on my side so I can watch the fire a little longer. "Thanks," I say and drift off while she strokes my hair.

MARA

When Dan fell asleep, I tried to ground him and clear him. His aura looked so frenzied, all the colors squished together in chaos rather than the pulsing rainbow ribbon that usually swirls around a person in a motion similar to a gentle flame.

I start with red, picture it in my mind, and that thought energy seems to pull the red out of the chaos and separate it. I separate all the colors like that so that when I'm all done, they look like the rainbow again instead of like a television when the station has gone off the air.

I set my alarm for a couple hours later, and when it goes off, I check on the young cows. I should have asked Daniel about what was going on out there. I walk near one cow on the ground, behind her so I can see how things are going, and there I see a tail coming out of her birth canal. My heart sinks. Daniel told me about this, but I've never actually seen it or dealt with it.

It's me against the contractions of a large Angus heifer. I have to push the calf back into the uterus and grab its back legs. It doesn't stand a chance of getting out butt first. I try not to think about having my arms up a cow's vagina or about being so close to where the poop comes out. I try to stay focused on the little life in there, the life that will be taken back in about ten months probably, but nonetheless, I feel like life needs a little victory these days, and that's what this is: me against death. I'm so tired of death. I stop pushing during the contraction and wait for it to pass, and then I push with all my might. I get nearly up to my shoulders and finally feel more space. I slide my hands around the calf, trying to identify what is what and, most of all, where the hind legs are. When I think I have both of them, I pull with all my might. I wedge my feet up against the cow and pull. She has more contractions. I keep pulling, and finally the calf slides out.

And then I started sobbing. I don't know why. Tears are funny like that. They don't always make sense. Maybe I'm simply overdue for a hard cry.

But, anyway, chalk one up for life. Finally.

DANIEL

I'm at a dance of some kind, sitting and watching. Mara is dancing like she means it, with a big smile on her face.

When the song is over, she approaches me. "Wanna give me another two-step lesson?" she asks. "I want to twirl."

"Not yet," I answer.

"How 'bout some food? I come here all the time, and the food is great."

"No, I just want to sit here," I reply.

"Suit yourself," and with that she goes off and dances again.

All of a sudden Grandma is there, and she gives me a little shake. "Wake up," she says, exasperated. "Honestly, Daniel," she mutters, "wake up." But I'm not ready.

Suddenly, I'm on the dance floor with my mom. "Hey, how'd you get me out of my chair?" I ask her.

"Desperate times call for desperate measures," she replies.

"Mothers have their ways. Hey, do I have to keep leading, or are you going to step up to the plate?" So I concentrate on leading. "Now listen to me. It wasn't your fault I died. It was my time. It was in my contract. You didn't do anything. So get on with it. Stop wasting your precious life. You have an important purpose on Earth, and with that happy times and many blessings will come your way if you're open enough to embrace them."

And just as suddenly as I found myself on the dance floor with Mom, I find myself in the buffet line with Dad. "What I want to say, son, is that you need to slurp up life like this here spaghetti. It's going to get all over your face sometimes and look like a mess, but, really, if you can get over appearances, it's good for you and it's tasty." He loads up my plate with more than I think I could eat in a week. "Here, boy, eat up. And then you go on and ask some girls to dance."

⚒

"I had a funny dream last night," I tell Mara the next day. "I was at a dance, and you were there and Grandma and my parents."

"Was I lookin' good?" she jokes.

"As usual," I reply, kidding her back.

"I had a dream that I was eating this really amazing spaghetti. Oh, Dan, it was so good, and I was just puttin' it down— practically double-fisting it—and it was getting all in my hair, but I didn't care." She smiles at me, almost as if she's waiting to see how I'll respond.

"Spaghetti, huh?" I ask, beginning to wonder about all of this. "My dad was trying to get me to eat spaghetti in the dream. Isn't that a coincidence?" I ask, hoping she'll say, Yes, what a strange coincidence.

But instead she says, "Well, you really should have because it was delicious."

MARA

I ask Dan if maybe we could go to the McRae house and see if there's anything we can do to make it more livable. He looks hesitant, but I pick up an empty box and a sage smudge stick.

We walk up the stairs together, past many black-and-white photos of straight-faced people, none of whom, I'm quite sure, are living today. We walk through the hall to his room. I take one step in and feel my lungs tighten. "Oh, I see," I say and take a step back.

"What?" Dan asked.

"Friend, you have a little psychic pollution problem here. We can clear it, but I'm wondering what will keep you from creating it all over again." He just looks at me, waiting for some cue, I guess. "Let's try this," I start as I light the sage. "Go to each corner of the room and fan the smoke. As you do, ask the Angels, silently if you want, to clear this room of all negative energies. Imagine them sweeping those energies out the window where they can be recycled into something positive. I'm going to go drink some water while you do that."

I figure he'd feel more comfortable doing what he needs to do without an audience. I'm sure I could do the same job in a quarter of the time he'll take, but it seems important that he do it. As I see it, action is thought taken one step further, so by taking action, regardless of what that action is as long as it relates to the thought, he commits to changing his thought patterns and makes new thought patterns concrete.

When I return, he is standing in the middle of his room, smoking sage stick in his hand, waiting for me. "Why don't you just set that on the windowsill?" I say, and he does. "What do you think about doing a little weeding in here?" I propose. He nods. "Okay, what would you like to create in your life?"

He looks at me uncomfortably.

"You don't have to share your answer. Just think about it. Okay, when you look at this room, what do you see?"

"The past," he replies without hesitating.

"Yes, and while the past has its place, it's kind of like button-weed in here, isn't it? Not much room for anything else." I hand him the empty box. "Make room for what you truly desire."

He packs his old toys and his old clothes. He folds up all the bedding and puts it in the hall. He takes down the curtains and rolls up the rug. He moves the pictures of his parents into the hall.

I take the lid off a big cardboard box. "You have a lot of negatives," I say as I look at its contents.

"Yeah," he says.

"Where are your prints?" I ask, thinking maybe something from that collection would be something he might like to bring in.

"I just have one—the one I made with you at the school. It's still in my grandparents' room," he says.

"You're telling me you have all these negatives and just one print? What's up with that?"

He shrugs. "I just like to have them."

Something about this isn't right. "Have the negatives? Or have your friends all tucked safely away in a box?"

He stops what he's doing and looks at me, maybe hurt or maybe just exposed. I can't tell. "Both," he finally says.

"Is it that you like to have them, or is it that you like to take them? Is taking someone's picture a way you show you care while still keeping something—your camera—between you and the people you care about?" I ask.

"Why are you asking me this? Why does it matter? Maybe I just like taking pictures," he says, still staring at me, confused.

"Or, sweetie, maybe the way you're relating to the world is affecting your happiness."

❦

We go into town and drop off his old toys at the thrift store. I spy an old aquarium in the corner. "Hey, how 'bout that?" I suggest, and he picks it up. We head next to the senior center, where some of the seniors propagate houseplants to sell, and then to the hardware store for paint. I watch him study the different colors and shades, and decide on gold. Last, we hit the fabric store for curtain fabric. He chooses green, blue, and gold flannel. We get enough to make a comforter cover, too. Then we go home and work some magic.

❦

In my dream I'm still in my own bed. I hear Heather Nova sing "Papercup," a waltz about how magical dancing is. Adam holds out his hand. I sit up and take it, joining him in a waltz. We dance and dance around my house until the song is almost over. He waltzes me back to bed. I sit, and then he kisses my hand before he disappears.

DANIEL

Minda, Paul, and Rob drive up the driveway right at sunset in their compact rental sedan. Rob's in the driver's seat, Paul shotgun, and Minda in the back.

Rob opens his door and shouts, "Howdy, partner!" He is wearing what I presume to be his new cowboy hat. He steps out and gives me a brotherly hug.

Paul gets out of the car and studies his surroundings. He brings his hand to his head as if to run his fingers through his hair, but since that's not an option, he just smoothes back his dreads. "Wild, man. This place is wild." His eyes look extra large in his big glasses.

"Paul was smart enough not to bring weed through airport security. He's still adjusting to not being stoned," Minda says as she climbs out of the backseat with a big brace on her leg. I help her. She hangs on me for a moment, and I hug her. "I can't do a lot with this thing on my leg, but I can cook," she says.

I kiss her cheek and whisper, "I'm so glad you're here." Then Rob hands her the crutches, and I have to let go.

I suddenly feel overwhelmed with relief.

A heifer in labor bellows out. "You're just in time for your lesson," I say to Paul and Rob.

Paul and Rob carry their bags into the house while I carry Minda's things. I have to change the plan and give her the downstairs room since I don't want her on stairs on crutches. I put Rob in my room and move my stuff to my grandparents' room.

Rob and Paul change while I grab a six-pack. On our way out to the maternity ward, we stop at the Church of the Dog so I can introduce them to Mara and ask her to go meet Minda. Then the guys and I tip back a couple while I teach them the ins and outs of calving—literally.

I tell them to come get me if they need me and head in for some much-needed sleep, leaving Rob and Paul to figure out things as they go.

When I walk up the stairs that night, I stop to take all the dead people off the wall.

MARA

After work, Minda and I press garlic cloves and sun-dried to-matoes into the dough and take it out to the oven. I mop out the cinders and shove the dough in on a big paddle. She tells me about skiing the backcountry of Alaska while I imagine it. I imagine the clarity up there.

Then our attention turns to Winter. "She's in heat," I explain to Minda. Winter squeals at Solstice and Pal. She squirts and backs up into them. She gives up, kicks one of the metal fence panels, and squeals some more. "The boys are gelded. They can't help her out. Sometimes I imagine that she's calling them pansies and sissies. She gets so mad at them for being gelded." Now and then Solstice raises his upper lip and holds his nose high in the air to tell her that he thinks she smells like Heaven, but he doesn't satiate her womanly desires. "She gets more and more frustrated and angry every day she's in heat," I say.

"I totally know how she feels," Minda says, looking over at the guys.

Paul starts the barbecue, Rob chops eggplant, zucchini, and portobello mushrooms, and Daniel sleeps on the porch swing. "Yeah, slim pickin's," I say.

"So you and Daniel aren't—?" she asks.

"Brotherlike friend," I say.

"Me, too," she says. "Though there are moments when I wonder . . ."

"He's a good guy. Knows how to dance. That's huge."

"Snores," she says.

"Oh, rats. No woman wants to sleep next to that," I say.

"Maybe for the right guy you just wear earplugs," she says.

Rob finishes chopping and leaves the vegetables in the olive oil and balsamic vinegar marinade I made. "Minda! Is it time for our surprise?" he calls over.

"Oh, you're going to love this!" she says to me. "Yes!" she squeals back to him.

"We discovered the farm and ranch supply store today!"

He runs to the backseat of the car and takes out five lengths of three-quarter-inch poly-propylene irrigation piping, each about twelve feet long, and five fittings. I don't get it. He unrolls the windows of the car and turns on an old B-52's CD. He gives each of us a piece of piping and a fitting. He can hardly contain his excitement.

The music wakes Daniel up, but he doesn't seem to mind.

Rob says nothing but inserts both ends of the twelve feet of pipe into the fitting. He struggles to get it in all the way. He holds it up for us to admire. Then he puts it over his head and begins to hula-hoop.

Minda cheers. She drops her crutches, picks up her pipe, does the same, jumps away from the picnic table on one foot, and joins Rob. Paul and I follow.

"Paul, it's a gentle motion! Use your legs!" Minda calls out over the music.

After several attempts he can keep the hula hoop up for a few minutes at a time.

And Daniel, you can guess, runs for his camera and takes our pictures.

In the distance, downdrafts from large, billowy spring storm clouds drop rain on faraway hills. In between our sun patch and that rain, a segment of rainbow forms. A rainbow—the beauty of the state of polarity between sorrow and light . . . life on Earth encapsulated.

We hula-hoop and watch the sky. And eventually we even talk Daniel into putting down his camera and joining us.

DANIEL

I ride out with Paul to check on the older cows and show him how to help the calves nurse when their old mothers have huge tits.

"I feel so dirty talking about tits like this," he says.

I give him a look.

The strong wind blows dust in our eyes. When we mount our horses again, I spot two coyotes feeding on a calf in a little ravine. The calf, still alive, calls out for its mother, who can't hear it on the wind. She stands on a ridge, looking around. The coyotes have eaten a back leg and have just broken into the stomach cavity. I pull out my gun and start shooting. I kill one coyote, but the other escapes. I ride over and shoot the calf.

Nearby I spot another coyote kill, a heifer who was having trouble delivering. The coyotes ate her butt right out.

Coyotes were here first. I know that. And mostly they eat rodents. I know that, too. I know there is supposed to be some kind of balance in nature, but you can't see this kind of carnage and not grow to hate them.

I turn around and look at Paul. His eyes are large. "Fuck," he says.

I reach into my saddlebag and hand him a beer.

MARA

That night the sound of Daniel shooting at a coyote woke me out of a dead sleep. The shot echoed twenty-one times in my head as I remembered standing in the ironic sunshine, my father's casket in front of me, covered with the American flag. I searched the expressionless faces of the men who fired their guns for some answer, some sense. I wanted to ask them, Was it worth it? Was a tiny country rich with oil really worth it? Why? Ultimately, though, no one can answer that for anyone else.

When I look at red, white, and blue, I think independence. Red, white, and blue are liars to me. There's no such thing as independence. I needed my dad.

DANIEL

"Come on, Daniel. Paul's got it covered. Two games, that's all we're asking," Minda says. It's hard to say no to her.

"I don't know, guys. I'm not very good at bowling," I say.

"Guys? He just called us 'guys,' Marge," Rob said to Minda. They're both wearing their thrift store bowling shirts. "You know when we don the shirts, you have to call us by our bowling names!" They point to the names embroidered on their shirts. "And it totally doesn't matter if you bowl well or not because I've got Hot Tamales! They make you bowl well!" Rob says, pulling out a box of cinnamon-flavored candy.

"Come on, Daniel. He's got Hot Tamales," Minda says. "We even have a surprise for you." She pulls a large green and black bowling shirt out of a plastic sack. She holds it up by the shoulders.

Rob points to the name. "We invite you to be Phil."

"Okay, Darrel. Okay, Marge. I'll be Phil," I say. I put the bowling shirt on over my white T-shirt.

"Sexy," Minda says and growls like a cat.

I put my arm around her and kiss the top of her head as we walk out the door.

MARA

In my dream, Gram and I float above Garden Valley High School, where two students shot ten others today. "Isn't it interesting what they've chosen to teach us?" she marvels.

"I don't know, Gram. This one hits a little close to home for me. That could've been me. I used to dream about hurting people like that."

"Oh, that never could have been you. You had too much compassion. I made sure of that." She dismisses my thoughts.

"Yes, I remember that night you took me to all the bullies' homes so I could see what they lived with. I was so mad at you for that because it completely disarmed me. All I had left to protect myself after that was my red aura." She taught me that as long as I pictured myself on fire, no one would touch me. She claimed I could walk down the streets of Harlem at night with a red aura, and no one would touch me. I've never felt the need to test that one.

"Well, did anyone actually touch you?" she challenges.

"No," I admit.

"Let's go join the others," she proposes. We float down to where there are spirit travelers like us, holding hands in circles like skydivers, only not falling. There are circles inside of circles of people like us, covering the whole town, here to clear the area with our love, here to send down healing energy, and here so that all those frightened people know on some level that they are being watched over.

The next day is a hard one for me. Children of all ages in all my classes speculate about what cupboards they could hide in if something like that happened in our school. The fears cloud the schools just like thick fog. At the elementary school I find out a troubled fifth grader brought a toy gun to school to scare all the kids in the cafeteria at breakfast, and later, at the high school, there's a bomb threat.

After school there's a staff meeting where this situation is discussed for five minutes before we are broken up into groups to brainstorm how to raise the test scores that already improved two hundred percent this year. I suggest better nutrition before I walk out.

I excuse myself as if I were going to the bathroom, but really I make a run for it—out of the school, across the parking lot, through the barbed wire fence, and up the hill to the place where the purple wildflowers grow. There, I try to clear the schools of all that fear and ask that it be recycled into something positive. I think about my participation in this institution that contributes more and more to breeding terrorists. I pray for clarity and direction.

I watch a hawk circle above me. Oka, an Onandoga friend of mine, believes hawks are messengers from Great Spirit, different from the way eagles are messengers but significant nonetheless. I watch the hawk and wonder what my message is.

In my dream, Gram brings Dad. I haven't seen him in at least a year, though from time to time I have the feeling he's checking in on me. He looks the same, so I would recognize him: hair the color of mine, piercing brown eyes, olive green flannel shirt, and Levi's. I give him a big hug.

"You know, I'm doubting this teaching business. I can't figure out if I'm part of the solution or part of the problem," I announce.

Dad nods silently for a minute. "Yes, you've done some damage," he confirms, and a few faces flash through my mind: Andy, Ashley, Brooke, Connor. And with each comes the instant knowing of what I did that hurt their feelings or embarrassed them. I feel mortified.

Then Dad projects us into the future. First, I see me building one-person churches for people. I seem pretty happy creating stained-glass windows on-site—not teaching. We flash to Kelli passed out in an alley. We flash to Kevin in the Navy, exposed to radiation. We flash to Brent, standing on a ledge. We flash to Cara dancing at a strip club. We see Nate get cut from minor league baseball and then go speeding down the freeway, weaving in and out of cars. We flash to Emily being held up at a mini-mart. We flash to Ty, unhappy in a cubicle in corporate America. Then we project into an alternate reality. Here, I am teaching. When I come home, a child comes running to greet me. We flash to Kelli, who is reading a story to a child on her lap. We flash to Kevin, doing massage therapy. We flash to Brent watching movies and cuddling with a loving partner on a couch. We see Nate and Cara opening their own art gallery together. We flash to Emily designing clothes in a hip loft in a city somewhere. We flash to Ty filming a movie in Hollywood.

All at once the slide show is over, and I am left by myself to make sense of it.

DANIEL

Grandma used to predict how much the steers would bleed by what she read in *The Old Farmer's Almanac*, and as much as Grandpa and I made fun of her for it, we could not deny she was right. She said when the moon was in any sign that ruled the heart to the head, there would be more bleeding, and when the moon was in a sign that ruled the knees on down, that was the best time for castration. For the steers, it's hit or miss. You can't wait for the right time in the cycle. For her horses, however, she would wait. I don't know what the moon is in today, but there is a lot of bleeding.

Tim and I rope and tie calves, Minda and Whitey brand, Hank and Paul castrate, and Mara and Rob vaccinate. After two days of this we've gotten into a good rhythm. I think we just may finish before Minda, Paul, and Rob leave tomorrow.

"Get up around Opal Lake yet?" Tim asks me. It used to be our favorite fishing spot. Big trout. Huge.

"Nah," I say.

"Well, if you find some really nice brown saddlebags out there, they're mine. And if you find them in the morning, there's a cold beer in them waiting for you. I lost most of my tack on one embarrassing incident I'd rather not tell about. I recovered everything but the saddlebags," he explains.

"Maybe the shepherds already found them," I say.

"I never considered the shepherds. That could be. I always figured it was the porcupines. I heard somewhere that they'll chew through your boots if you let them," he says as he moves a few more calves into the chute.

"Really?" I close a gate.

"Oh, yeah. They love leather," he says.

At the end of the day Hank and Whitey cook steaks over the branding iron fire. Paul and Rob sit near them.

"Smells good," Rob says.

"I can't smell anything over Medusa's hair," Hank says.

Whitey turns to Paul. "You gotta cut that hair, Medusa."

"No woman is ever going to get near you with hair that smells like that," Hank says.

Paul takes it like a good sport.

"This is an intervention, Paul. Those dreads are a lifetime sentence of celibacy!" says Rob.

Mara prepares something in a skillet with one of those big mushrooms and tofu. It looks disgusting to me. Tim sits between her and Minda.

I take the salad and bread out of the back of the pickup and make a buffet on the tailgate. Everyone is starved.

"They're ready," Whitey says. "Get your plates."

Tim tries to hit on both Mara and Minda. "I don't care

whether a woman is fat or thin. I've had a lot of fat girlfriends. I believe you have to appreciate whatever a woman has," he says like he simply loves women. "Until that bitch gets mouthy," he says as he gets up to get another beer. Minda and Mara blink with shock and exchange horrified glances.

"It's a wonder he's been divorced twice, isn't it?" Whitey says.

"I can't believe we pulled this off," I say, looking out over the ranch and then back at everyone. And that's when I realize I could never sell this place. This ranch is more than land and cattle and my past. This ranch is family and stories and community and who I have become. I look at all my friends and blink back my gratitude. "Thank you all so much for being here. Here's to you." I lift my beer.

"Cheers," everyone says.

I like to think Grandpa is watching and that he's proud of us.

I assemble my tripod and camera, and this time I jump into the picture with everyone else.

❧

Minda slides a smoked salmon and green onion omelet onto a plate for me. I am going to miss her cooking. Actually, I'm just plain going to miss her. "Are you going to be okay here without us?" she asks.

"Yeah," I say even though I don't want them to go.

Paul descends the stairs, drops his bag, and joins us in the kitchen. "Coffee. Must have coffee," he says like a caveman, and he makes his way to the coffeepot. "Rob! Robert! Roberto! Come on, buddy. The clock is ticking!"

Rob comes down the stairs, sets his bag down near the door, and sits at the kitchen table with us. "Oh, Minda's omelets! Heck yes!"

"Hey, listen, guys, I have something to tell you," I say. "I realized yesterday that I can't sell this place."

Minda looks down at her coffee cup, Paul keeps his eyes on his omelet, but Rob looks directly at me. "You'd be an idiot to sell this place."

I smile at him and nod, appreciative of his support.

"Can I come back for branding next year?" he asks.

"I'll count on it," I say.

"I'll come back, too," Paul says. He takes another bite and says, "Man, we're going to miss you."

"Aren't you going to be lonely here?" Minda asks.

"Sometimes," I say. "But there's a lot of people here who care about me."

"But aside from Mara, I don't really see any female companion prospects for you here," she says.

"You mean you're not going to come back and marry me?" I only half-joke.

"Well, I'll think about it, but the skiing isn't very good here," she says.

"No, not right here," I admit. "You know, Alaska wasn't crawling with prospects, either. I think my odds are actually better here. All I have to do is put the word out, and everyone in town would be looking for prospective brides for me." I laugh just picturing the church ladies calling all their out-of-town relatives to see if they know anyone. It happens.

"If you get lonely, come up and visit us, okay?" Minda says.

"I'll be up in a month to pack up my room and clean," I say.

"He's going to clean?" Rob says, alarmed.

"Dear God," Paul says with concern and awe.

"I'll help you," Minda offers.

"That's love," Rob says. "I, for one, will be glad to be on the boat by then."

"Amen," Paul agrees.

"We'll get through it together," Minda says to me. "Okay, cowboys, time to load up and head out."

Paul and Rob shove the rest of their food in their mouths, get up, and pick up their bags. I pick up Minda's suitcase and walk them all to their car. Paul and Rob each give me a quick hug, say good-bye, and get in the car. Minda puts her crutches in the backseat and then gives me her good-bye hug.

"If you need anything, anything at all, don't hesitate to call me, okay? I'll be around this summer. I can be here if you need me," she says.

I kiss her cheek as I let her go. "You're the best, Minda. Thanks. Thanks for being here." Then I tousle her hair like I would a little sister. "Go catch your plane."

"Much love to you, sweet guy," she says as she touches her heart.

"Much love to you, too," I say back. I've never said *love* to anyone other than my grandparents or parents before. I'm surprised how naturally it came out.

She gets in the car and shuts the door. Rob backs it up, turns it around, and drives away down the driveway. I hold up my arm and wave as they go. My stomach hurts. I want to cry, but I don't. Instead, I turn around, take a deep breath, and think about chores to distract myself. And for the first time I seriously consider letting the church ladies fix me up.

MARA

Something interesting is happening. My students have started traveling with me in the dream realm at night.

Take last night, for example. I don't know where I was. In my dream I was walking down a busy street in one of those skimpy tennis outfits with my tennis racket on my way to go play tennis. That's all I remember. It struck me as odd since I don't play tennis.

I didn't think much more about it until Emily came in seventh period and said, "Oh, Ms. O'Shaunnessey, I had the funniest dream last night. You, me, Kevin, and Nate were all playing tennis. Then my mom came to pick me up, and I had to go."

"Was I any good at it?" I ask.

"Well, you and I beat the boys," she replies, pleased with herself.

I smile. "I had a dream I was walking to tennis courts in a tennis outfit and with a racket. I was walking down a four-lane busy street. Do you know where we were?"

"No."

"Let's ask Kevin if he remembers his dream. Don't tell him about yours until we see what he says."

A few minutes later Kevin comes to class. "Hey, Kevin, do you remember your dream last night?" Emily asks him.

He thinks, says, "Oh, yeah," and laughs. "I dreamt I threw a tennis ball at a moose and knocked it out."

Nate didn't remember his dream, but I've had several travel dreams with Nate in them. Once he even showed up in the Church of the Dog in hologram form in the middle of the night. He never remembers.

In my dream I'm driving this other teacher's minivan down the road, singing "This Little Light of Mine" at the top of my lungs. I pass a bicyclist and wave. That's it. I wake up and think what a stupid dream, but when I see that teacher at work, I tell her about it anyway, expecting her to find it funny.

Instead, she looks at me, puzzled, and says, "That's so weird, because I have this tape of a gospel choir singing that song, and it's the kids' favorite. We listen to it all the time in the car and sing along."

DANIEL

I am eight years old in Dad's sixty-four green Ford pickup, comfortably squished between my parents. The first snow has begun to fall, coating the icy road that winds around the canyons between Pendleton and Three Hills. Mom begins to sing "Let It Snow" in exuberance because in the quiet winter Dad gets a break from planting and harvesting wheat for two or three short months, and we all get to spend time together.

The snowflakes get thicker, hitting our windshield one after another. Dad creeps along, straining to see through the thick waves of snow. "Oh, God" is the last thing he says before Mom throws herself in front of me. We hit the deer, bounce off, slide and spin on the ice, and then roll over the edge of the highway and down, down, down. Time slows. Mom grips me tighter, sheltering me with her whole body. I smell the carnation perfume Dad and I gave her for her birthday just weeks before. The truck rolls one, two, three, a hundred times before it comes to rest on its roof. I close my eyes and don't move, still engulfed in my mother's embrace. My parents are silent and still. I keep my eyes shut.

The next morning I open my eyes to see myself completely covered in blood, though I don't know whose. Grandpa calls to us from the road high above. This is when I scream. I scream and scream, shaking in my mother's cold embrace. I don't remember what happened after that.

It occurs to me that if Mara is right: If this camera is how I relate to the world, maybe I need to go back to that moment when my life changed. Maybe I need to photograph that and make some sense of it.

Today I drive out the old road that goes to Pendleton and stop where we went off the edge. I park on the other side, the side that cuts into the hill. I get out and take a picture of the place. I stand at the top and imagine how Grandpa must have felt looking down at the Ford. I half-run, half-slide down the hill as he must have done, past the shards of our shattered windows, still there after all this time. I see an old tailpipe and photograph it. At the bottom I stop near what was left of the old Ford. They never figured out how to get it out of there.

I sit down for a while and talk to Mom and Dad until I sob. I tell them about all the guilt I've had for so long as the only survivor, the one who survived because his mother sheltered him, took the blows for him, gave her life for him.

I tell them how my life has been, how I've run away from everything—everything from the circuit finals to love—and how now my life is so empty, and I feel just as numb as I did the moment they left. I tell them how worthless a life like this is to me, and I ask them, if they can hear me, if they would please help me change it, if they would please help me find my way, if they would please help me experience love. I sit, arms around myself, and rock back and forth, eyes closed, remembering how it felt to be with them, remembering their comfort.

After a while—I have no idea how long—I get up, photograph the old Ford from several angles, and finally make my way back up to the road.

MARA

In my dream Earl shows up in mechanic's overalls. "Listen, tell Dan that his problem is his second fuel filter. It's under the front wheel well. He'll need a special tool to get to it."

Whitey and Dan are working on Dan's Ford pickup. I hear Whitey mumble "dadgum" a lot.

"Hey," I say. "I had this dream last night where Earl told me to tell you that the problem lies in your second fuel filter. He said it's under the wheel well, and you'll need a special tool to get to it."

Of course they laugh at me. "Second fuel filter?" they say, puzzled. "Ever hear of a second fuel filter?" Lots of head shaking, and then when they think I'm not looking, they check under the wheel well.

Dan is on his way to NAPA to get a new fuel filter for an '88 Ford 250 and the special tool to install it.

❧

Of all the teachers that intrigue me, I think the kindergarten and first-grade teachers intrigue me most. They are a different breed. They are, more than any others, the teachers of conformity, discipline, and structure. Yet they are also perhaps the most sensitive and kind. While I do not value conformity or structure, and this is an understatement, I believe these people must've thrived in it, were successful at it, and want to share the joy of conformity and structure with others. What amuses me is how they are commanding with soft, gentle, patient voices.

Sally is leaving the building at the same time I am. "Sally," I say, "I'm going to build a Harley, and on the day I retire, I'm going to wear black leather shorts that are entirely too revealing and ride away to Sturgis." I say *retire*, but I really mean "get fed up and leave this institution."

"Dean and I had a bike. In fact, we rolled into here on it. It was a Honda. Harleys are too bumpy. When you get to be my age, you think about bladder control and take the smoothness of a bike into consideration. When I think of Harleys, I think of bump, leak, bump, leak, bump, leak." She giggles at her own candidness.

There is nothing about her Dorothy Hamill hairdo, big glasses, and teacher jumper that prepares me for her biker identity. "Yes, Dean marveled at me as we drove cross-country because he'd never seen anyone sleep on the back of a bike before. I slept through most of Arizona!" She giggles again.

"No way, Sally! You were a biker?"

She giggles and nods.

"Sally, did you sport the black leather ensemble?"

"No, brown."

"Fringe?"

"Not on my biker coat, but I did have a vest with fringe down to my knees and beads on the ends of the fringe."

"I have a vest with long fringe on the bottom. I like to wear it while dancing around the house to 'The Best of War.' "

I laugh and she giggles. "Yes, I was quite involved in the anti-war movement. I demonstrated a lot and even got arrested." She holds up two fingers and says, "Twice." It's just what you'd expect from a first-grade teacher, which cracks me up. "I was Jane Doe number thirty-one," she tells me with a proud, mischievous smile. "Don't tell. Even my husband doesn't know." She grabs my elbow for emphasis.

Being the new person in town is fun. People are relieved to find a secret keeper, someone with no connections, no link to the gossip network. Thus, we newcomers get an intimate peek into the secret lives of small towns.

I look at her jumper with apples on it. Every teacher in America, except me, has a variation of it. I think maybe they are issued with teaching certificates, and I wasn't sent one due to some processing error. Sally, in her apple jumper, a former protesting biker who spent time in the pokey and wore long fringe. I never, ever would have guessed.

"Have a good night!" she calls to me in her soft, perky, first-grade-teacher voice as she goes her own way. I think she knows she just made my night.

DANIEL

I drive to the church to photograph it from the perspective of an eight-year-old looking up at it from the sidewalk. I walk to the footbridge, photograph it, crawl under it, and photograph my world from there. I walk on across town to the cemetery, see Dawson outside the coffee shop along the way, and photograph him from across the street. I walk up the hill, through the gates, and to the old willow tree I stood under when they put my parents in the ground. I photograph their stone and the tree. I go on to photograph the grave of Grandpa and Grandma, which still doesn't have grass growing over it yet.

I go on home to develop the film and to make prints.

I look at my prints closely as they hang from clothespins in the darkroom. I study them as if the prints might hold some clue I had never noticed, some clue that would finally make it all make sense. They don't.

MARA

Since the overlapping dream, we all come into seventh period and compare notes about who dreamed what.

"You know, Ms. O'Shaunnessey, I have this recurring dream where I'm in my room, and I can't turn on the lights and I can't open the door. I feel freaked out, but I know if I just go back to bed, everything will be okay," Kate tells me during one of our dream conversations.

I pull her aside and say quietly but with a smile, "You're traveling. Next time, look behind you for a silver cord that attaches you to your body. If you see it, you don't need to open the door, girl, 'cause you can go anywhere you want. It's fun. Explore it."

She looks at me like I'm nuts but seems interested.

"I go all over the place," I tell her and then walk off.

I remember when I was very little and first became aware that I was traveling. I'd clean my fingernails really well before bed every night. I was thinking that if there was dirt in them the next morning, it would prove I had gone somewhere. I don't remember if I ever found any dirt. Isn't that a funny thing for a little kid to do?

DANIEL

About fifty people show up at the library to see my black-and-white photographs. The place where we crashed. The tailpipe. The old Ford. The church. The footbridge I hid under. Dawson, the police officer. Their graves. The ceiling of my bedroom. Their portraits hanging in the hall. Some photos of me being whipped around by a bull, then thrown. Then phase two: portraits of my grandparents, the church, Father McCleary, their fresh graves, me being scooped up by the horns of a bull, me airborne, me being crushed by the bull, a look of pain and surrender on my face under his hooves. I call my show "Images from an Orphan."

Whitey is dressed up for the occasion in his blue cowboy jacket and lapis bolo tie. I approach him from behind and stand next to him. He peers at me below his deeply hooded eyelids. " 'Images from an Orphan,' huh? Is that what you really think you are? You fool. You ought to take a picture of everyone in this room"—he points around—"of everyone in this blessed town and hang them up and call them Family Portraits. You ought to have pictures of me distracting that bull before he ran you over." He stares me down for a minute, clearly disgruntled. "Going on pretending you're a dagblame orphan when all these people raised you, when I raised you." His eyes water just a little. "What are you trying to tell me? I'm not family?" He turns and walks out.

And it hits me what I've done. "Whitey," I call after him apologetically. He just swats his hand backwards, without turning around, in a motion of complete disgust, as if trying to shoo me away.

SUMMER

MARA

I want to do a tribute to Edith. I want to do a tribute to our Lady Godiva runs.

Everywhere you go out here there is metal junk just rusting in people's rangelands. It's junk to most people, but to me it's art waiting to happen. How would I know about all this metal junk, you ask? I confess I am a trespasser. I like to explore, sometimes naked, and I like the unlawful act of trespassing just for the thrill of being naughty—well, that and my belief that no one really owns the land. They only agree legally to take care of it. Some of them are doing a mighty poor job, I might add. Anyway, I figure my trespassing doesn't hurt anyone.

Lately, the thrill of trespassing has proven not to be enough. That metal calls to me. It wants to be art. It wants to be my tribute to Edith. I don't want to haul it anywhere. See where I'm going with this? Doing the art on-site seems appropriate for the person and the act I am paying tribute to.

It's the week of the summer solstice, and the moon is full. I'm caught up in the freedom of summer.

I pack my headlamp, a small propane torch, two extra tanks of propane, solder, flux, a pad of steel wool, a saw, wire clippers, a metal awl, a hammer, pliers, and a camera. I put it all in a saddlebag on Solstice and mount up. I plan to make these creations near the path Edith and I used to ride into town. I ride out through the golden grass, through a field of alfalfa, purple blossoms sitting atop rich green stems and leaves, and back into the golden grass again.

Site one is the smallest metal scatter but the closest. I assemble chunks of metal together to suggest a voluptuous woman form with one foot slightly forward and her upper body leaning back. Her arms are up, with palms facing the sky. I clip some barbed wire that had been lying on the ground nearby and use it for strands of her hair. I use bullet casings for a necklace. I photograph my masterpiece, pick up, pack up, mount up, and gallop across two small ridges to site two.

Site two is a large metal scatter from a tractor breakdown. Over the next three and a half hours I transform it into a woman on a horse. I must tell you that designing this so it will balance, even in strong winds, is no easy feat. I'm not really counting on these sculptures lasting very long. Propane isn't the ideal way to go, and the metal is rusty. That is why I'm photographing them.

By now it's much lighter than I anticipated. I fear someone will see me leave the area, and my art will no longer be anonymous. But before I go, I take a photograph, pause, and look at it. I think I hear Edith laugh. I go home in a roundabout way and fall into bed.

The rest of my week goes much like this at night except that due to travel time I usually can do only one sculpture a night. By the end of the week I've completed ten. All the sculptures are women or horses, though one is of a woman and a man waltzing. Even though I don't expect them to last long, I hope before they fall some ranchers will find my sculptures and be surprised and amused by the fruits of my deviance. They won't recognize the sculptures as Edith, but they'll be touched by the spirit of the sculptures, and that spirit is Edith.

DANIEL

Minda and I took four trips to the dump in Valdez and now face the kitchen in our rain gear and ventilators. "I think we should take the refrigerator outside before we clean it," she proposes, "since the EPA has declared it a level five biohazard. We don't want to turn those microbes loose in the house!" We rock the fridge back and forth, inching it out to the back porch.

"You know, I think we should just take it to the dump," I say. "Who knows what kind of bleach-resistant strain of E. coli might be in there? You guys could die. I don't want that tragedy on my hands. I think you guys should pick up a used one for ninety bucks and not take the risk."

"Hm. You're probably right." We rock the fridge onto a dolly, roll it over to my truck, and load it on its side. We return to the house. "Is anything eating through the grease on the walls?" Minda has test patches on the kitchen walls for 409, Citrisolve, and oven cleaner.

"Nothing yet," I reply. "Maybe it just needs more time."

"Hey, what about S.O.S. pads?"

"You want to S.O.S. the kitchen walls?"

"We're going to have to scrub them anyway." She surrenders to the kitchen. We moisten our S.O.S. pads and start scrubbing.

"I wish Gopher was here," she says with a sigh. Since Rob is back working on cruise ships, Minda has started in with the *Love Boat* references. "He would know what music to choose right now."

"You underestimate me." I pretend I'm offended. "I didn't live with you all for the last five years and not learn something."

"Really!" She waits.

"Donna Summer, 'She Works Hard for the Money.' " I grin.

"Genius," she whispers and runs off to find it.

"Oh, I forgot to give you this. Paul would've never forgiven me. When he got home from Oregon, he cut off all his dreadlocks and made key chains out of them for his friends." She opens her hand. There is one of Paul's dreads attached to a key chain with a wire. Two plastic googly eyes are glued to the dreadlock. It smells. The problem with dreadlocks in a wet climate is that they never dry and eventually mold. Paul's head always smelled just slightly better than the black mildew in the shower.

"Oh, he really shouldn't have," I reply. "I'm just going to put this outside." When I return, Minda is scrubbing away at the kitchen wall to Donna Summer.

"So what, may I ask, ever became of Herb?"

"Oh, yes, Herb. Rob vetoed him."

As we scrub and scrub, I realize how much we were a family here in this house and how much I miss them. "You know, you guys can come down and visit me anytime you want. Stay as long as you want. If you ever get sick of skiing, you could be a full-time cowgirl."

"Sick of skiing? That's funny," she says with an exaggerated laugh. "I have to make up for lost time now that my knee has healed."

"You guys are family, you know." I take a moment and look her in the eye.

"Yeah, I know," she replies tenderly and puts her dishwashing glove–covered hand around my back, leaving a blue S.O.S. soap handprint on my raincoat. She rests her head on my shoulder for a minute.

I kiss the top of her head.

MARA

I left my home, Solstice, Harvey, and Zeus in the hands of Casey, one of my students who I'm hoping will not host a party while I'm gone, and drove south. I wanted to take Zeus but was afraid it would be too hot in the truck for him. I figured he would be more comfortable at home. I think Casey will take good care of him.

It's a year since my last trip here, and I play my guitar on the canyon rim, hoping that if it's meant to be, Adam will hear me. But the sun rises, and I am still alone.

I woke at 4:00 a.m. to drive here from just north of Flagstaff, and if you've ever driven that road, you know it's covered by mule deer. The drive was hairy, and last night I didn't sleep very well, wondering what this morning would bring, and all this leaves me feeling quite tired. Since I don't roll around in my sleep or anything, I figure I'll just lie right here on the edge of the canyon and take a nap.

As I come out of my sleep, I hear many voices, some of which say things like "Nice place to take a nap" and "Don't roll over!" I open my eyes to see a little girl, about five years old and dressed in a cowgirl outfit, standing over me waving a magic wand. More and more I become aware that there are hundreds of people walking by me.

I get up as fast as I can, grab my guitar, which I can't believe is still there given the circumstances, and begin to bolt when my eye catches Adam, tucked in the juniper, laughing at me.

"I figured I'd catch you if you started to roll," he says with a smile.

"Hello, old friend," I greet him.

"Shall we go to a quieter part of the canyon?" he proposes.

"If one exists!"

He holds out his hand, and I take it.

We stop by my truck so I can drop off my guitar and grab my day pack. Then we stop a little ways away where he parked his VW Bus so he can get his. We begin our hike west along the south rim. First, we have to pass all the hotels, tour buses, and mobs of people.

"You know, I hoped I would see you again, but I didn't expect it to happen so soon," he confesses. "I thought about you from time to time, which is funny, I guess, considering I only knew you for fifteen minutes or so." His aura really flames out. It's huge. The rainbow spirals around him at a nice, healthy speed, very regularly and rhythmically.

"You did more than think about me. Don't you remember visiting?"

"You remember?" He smiles. "A lot of people don't remember."

"You're a good dancer," I say, and we laugh. "And in reality you've probably known me for more than fifteen minutes."

He nods, as if to say, "Yes, probably so," but instead asks, "Do you remember anything?"

"You mean like past lives?" I ask.

"Yes."

"No," I reply.

"Me, neither." He sounds disappointed about that.

"I figure if we were supposed to, on a more conscious level anyway, we would."

"Probably so," he consents.

That evening when we return to the parking lot, he gets his ice chest, and we find a picnic table. He lights a couple candles and puts hurricane lamps around them. Then he brings out hummus and pita for appetizers while he starts frying up falafel.

"Vegetarian?" he asks me.

"That obvious?" I laugh, and he nods. "Hey, do you ever look in people's carts at the grocery store and imagine what their colons look like?" I ask.

"Of course," he replies without thinking. I laugh some more. This leads us to a conversation about the virtues of garlic.

When dinner is over and we've packed up, he walks me to my truck and gives me a piece of paper with his address and phone number on it. "I'm not hard to find," he says.

"Me, neither," I reply, and write down my address to give to him. "I have no phone, so if you want to visit, you just have to show up."

"Is that an invitation?" he asks.

"Yes," I say.

"Then I'll see you again." With that he gives me a very, very nice kiss. I get in my pickup, he gets in his Bus, and as we drive off in our separate directions, something deep in my gut tells me it's wrong. It's wrong to be parting ways.

ÐANIEL

I spent the last three days in my darkroom, this time making proof sheets of all my negatives and actually making prints. At Minda's urging I took a handful of my favorites to her friend Sue who owns a gallery down on the waterfront where the cruise ships dock. Sue was really excited about three shots in particular: my shipmates hauling up crab pots; our captain's face as we tied up, safe after a particularly frightening storm; and Paul sorting through the nets in pouring rain. She asked me to bring more prints down today, so I print ten each of twenty photographs for starters. She said if people buy these, I can always print more in Oregon to send up.

While I was at it, I picked my five favorite shots of the housemates to print, frame, and leave on the living room wall as a good-bye present. In the first, Minda and Rob are dancing to Sly and the Family Stone in Afro wigs that Rob picked up for them in Seattle. The second is of Paul up in the old maple tree. I took it when he went through his arboreal phase where he slept in trees in order to get back to his early primate roots. His dreadlocks blend with the moss that hangs from the branches. The third is a rear view of Rob on the back patio striking a John Travolta pose, with a black bear running away in the distance. The fourth is of the night they all fell asleep together on the floor watching movies. And the last one was taken on the day we branded and castrated cattle. They're all making sadistic faces while they hold up their respective tools: Minda with the branding iron, Paul with a knife, and Rob with a syringe. I have roped all of them and hold them in my lasso. Mara took that shot. It makes me laugh every time I look at it.

I take a minute to view all my prints hanging in the red light and soak them up. It feels like my view of the world has finally come to maturity. In each photograph I finally see my family.

❦

Back in Oregon I wander around the Three Hills Library once again, looking at the faces of those looking at my photographs, this time in color. There is tenderness as they laugh at some and carefully examine others. There is a photo of Whitey leaning on a fence and pointing out something in the distance. Owen on top of his tractor. Bertha bringing me a plate of cookies in her kitchen. Hank moving cattle with me, mouth open—in the middle of a story, no doubt. The list goes on. I called this collection, which I'm donating to the Three Hills Historic Museum, "Our Family Portraits."

Whitey approaches me from behind and gives me a one-arm hug from the side. "You done good, boy," he says with a wink. But it was his proud smile that really said it all.

"Thanks, Uncle Whitey," I responded. "Thanks for everything."

MARA

I walk down the driveway to the mailbox. Inside is a box and a letter for me. I run all the way back up the driveway to the picnic table outside my little house.

First, I tear into the box. It's from Gram. I open it to find my lily bulbs, sprouted, and iris tubers with greenery all wrapped in wet paper towels and plastic wrap. I take out her note and read it: "While your soul is welcome to reside in my garden always, don't you think it's time you plant a little of your soul where you are?"

Then I pick up the plain white envelope addressed to me from Triumph, Idaho. I resist the urge to tear into it as fast as I can. Instead, I take it out behind the Church of the Dog, back where the sunflowers grow, and sit among them, cross-legged.

As I tear open the flap, I consider how his tongue had been there, and I find that strangely exciting.

I pull out the plain white paper and take in his handwriting—printing, not cursive. Intuitive. I knew that. Thankfully, he doesn't use all capitals, either. People who use all capitals are either hiding something or so deep inside themselves that I'll never get them out. Yes, I'm relieved to see he uses lowercase letters. His letters are pretty straight up and down, not an emotional right slant or a try-not-to-be-emotional left slant. The loops on his g's and y's are incomplete: incomplete sex life. He uses blue ink instead of black, and I can't tell you why, but I like that. Something about blue ink is friendlier. He crosses his t's in the right place and without an abusive slant. His signature is consistent with the rest of his writing rather than being an entirely different penmanship style, which means that he is who he appears to be. He writes quickly. A quick thinker. I like that.

After I look at it, I read it.

> *Dear Mara,*
>   *I can't stop thinking about you. Would you be up for*
> *a visit from me? I'd like to get to know you better.*
>   *Yours,*
>   *Adam*

After I read it, I smell it. It smells like nothing.

And then I get excited. I fan myself with it as I smile and make excited squeals that are totally out of character for me to make.

I get up and run into the Church of the Dog, get my bright yellow paper and a pen and a book to write on, and then run back to the sunflowers.

Dear Adam,
   I can't stop thinking about you, either. Get in your
bus and drive to Oregon right now.
   Yours,
   Mara

I fold it once, put it in the envelope, lick it, kiss it, and study his envelope to address it. Then I stand up again, run back into the Church of the Dog for a stamp, and do a little dance. Actually, I do a big dance. I stop and make myself take some deep breaths, but I can't help but to keep shaking the excitement out of my hands.

I take the grocery list off my door and write *wine* on it. "Please let him be everything I think he is!" I say and then catch myself. "Cancel that. Please let me have the clarity and intelligence to see who he really is instead of being blinded by who I hope he is. Let me have the courage to see the truth and accept it. Whatever the outcome, let the journey be fun and not destructive to me in any way." That's better. I take a few more deep breaths and settle down.

Still, it's an adventure, and I love adventures, whether they are geographical or adventures of the heart. Adventures are exciting, and I always learn something.

❦

I knock on Daniel's door, and when he opens it, I say, "I'm long overdue for my second two-step lesson. I'm afraid I'm the only person in these parts who doesn't know how to do it reasonably fast and how to twirl."

"Nah, there are other people who don't know." He doesn't get my hint.

"Well, what I'm getting at," I say, "is that while I was hoping for a gay male friend to take me dancing every weekend as I move gracefully into spinsterhood, I was thinking maybe you'd do." I try to charm him with a smile.

"Oh, really?" he replies, somewhere between amused and offended, I think.

"Yes. Assuming you're a decent dancer," I challenge.

"Oh, I'll show you!" He mocks my challenge but gets up and picks—I swear—the fastest song he could find, something I didn't recognize, involving yodeling. He returns and extends his hand to me. I get up, and he takes me for a spin I won't soon forget. By the time we were done, I didn't know which end was up because of all the spins he took sadistic joy in making me do.

When the song ends, we notice Zeus barking at the door. I thought he was just barking at all the excitement going on in the house, but he is going nuts about something outside. Dan and I freeze for a moment to listen.

"Sounds like a dying rabbit or maybe a coyote," Dan says and shuts off the music on the way to the door. When he cracks the door to peer outside, Zeus pushes his way through and runs to the Church of the Dog. "Hey, you'd better come with me," Daniel says warily, so I get up from the table, a little afraid.

It takes me a minute to put it all together, what I'm seeing and hearing. As we walk toward my house, a pastel blob begins to take the shape of a newborn baby in a car seat. We reach the porch, and I just stand there looking down at this foreign little thing. I don't know anything about babies. I don't even know how to hold them. Its hysterical crying assaults my nervous system so that instinct takes over, and soon I pick up the little one in her fuzzy, pink blanket with bunnies on it, in an attempt to make it stop.

Dan and I look at each other, bewildered, as if asking each other if this is really happening. And I don't know, sometimes my humor comes out at the most inappropriate times: "What do you think, Dan? Does motherhood become me?" I joke, pretending I accept the circumstances.

He gives me a look like he can't believe I'm joking when this child has just been abandoned. His breath becomes forced as he looks at the child, like he would reach for a window if he weren't already outside.

Dan begins to go through the yellow vinyl diaper bag with Big Bird on it and a million pockets, pulling out diapers, a few clothes—mostly pink—and from another pocket a bunch of papers. He looks at one. "Birth certificate. Her name is Faith." He unfolds another. " 'Ms. O'Shaunnessey, I thought I could be different than my mom, but I'm not. She wouldn't stop crying, so I hit her. She's two months old and I hit her.' " Dan stops reading for a minute and takes a deep, forced breath. " 'I want her to have better. I used to sit in class and wonder what it would've been like if you were my mom. That's what I want for her. Kelli.' " Dan pauses for a minute, then looks up and asks, "So Kelli was your student?"

"Yeah. The girl with the black eye at the parade. Fifteen years old. Dan, I have no idea what to do now."

He shakes his head as if to say he's just as lost as I am.

"Dan, people don't leave babies on doorsteps. Okay, maybe in books and movies, but not in real life. This doesn't happen in real life. Real life is more complicated. There are legal matters, you know? I can't just keep her. How do I keep her without being suspected of kidnapping? Or having the state take her away from me and stick her in a foster home? See, you have to think of these things!"

I'm starting to freak out as the reality of this situation sinks in. But as I bounce up and down with the child in my arms, I must admit that something about holding a baby feels very fundamental and natural to me, as if the baby were filling a hole in my chest, a hole in my heart.

I watch something shift in Dan that I can't really explain, but the words that follow this change in demeanor surprise me. "You know, Mara, I'm just starting to get it that the way a person's family takes shape is not always what they expected. What I'm saying is, maybe this is all exactly how it's supposed to be." He kind of glances at the sky to imply this is God's plan.

"But, Dan, I have no clue what to do with this."

"Give yourself some credit, Mara. Jesus, you mother everything on this ranch from plants and hogs to sick cows. I think you're ready. I think you'll be a good mom."

"Yeah, but see the difference here is that I can't leave a baby in the barnyard while I'm at work. I never wanted to be in this situation. I never wanted to raise a child by myself."

"I thought you said you were my family," he says.

"Yes," I answer.

"Then I'm yours, too. You wouldn't have to raise a child by yourself."

"God, you're serious, aren't you?" I take a minute and look at him like he's crazy.

"Absolutely," he replies slowly and with confidence.

"But, Dan, you and I aren't the only people involved here. What about Kelli? What if she just needs help learning different ways to handle stress? Can you imagine living with something like this? I want to give her a chance to do it right, you know, to try it again—with a little support this time."

He considers this. "You know, to use your garden analogy, it sounds like she's got a lot of weeding to do before she'll have space for a baby. I don't think that kind of weeding can happen overnight, you know? I think she did the right thing."

Zeus catches a scent and takes off down the driveway. Dan-

iel and I look at each other. Faith's crying escalates to screaming. I hand Daniel the baby and race down the long driveway
behind Zeus. I run and run into the strong wind, even as Zeus
turns into a smaller and smaller white dot. Far down below, the
taillights on a car parked at the end of the driveway reflect red
light as another car drives past, and I realize Kelli is somewhere
between those lights and me and that if I can reach her before
she drives away, we'll have one outcome, and if I can't, we'll all
be stuck with an outcome that will ultimately be much harder
for both her and Faith to live with. The driveway is full of ruts
and potholes, so I try to focus on each stride, but all I can think
is, What if I don't get to her in time? And that thought slows everything down like in those dreams where you want to run but
you can't. Every second that all our fates hang in the balance
seems like an unbearable infinity. I have time to consider all the
ways our lives might look one year from now, five years from
now, ten years from now, and twenty years from now based on
whether I reach Kelli before she gets to her car and whether I
can convince her to stay once I do reach her. Eventually, the
tiny white dog that is Zeus begins to get bigger, and I realize
he has stopped, but still I keep running. I run all the way up
to the larger and larger white dot until I see Kelli sitting in the
driveway, crying. I run all the way up to her, but she doesn't
look at me.

I crouch next to her. "Hey," I say softly. "Hey, what's going
on?"

All she does is sob loudly. She bends over her legs, her face
in her hands, and she sobs loudly.

"Hey," I say again and rub her back a little. "Hey, no matter
how bad it seems now, it's going to be okay. I'll help you. But
you gotta tell me what's going on."

She can't. She sits up, my arm still on her back, and puts her head into my shoulder and sobs. "I just can't do it!" she finally gets out.

I realize I'm going to be here awhile, so I sit down next to her and embrace her, so grateful she didn't actually leave.

"I'm just like my mom!" she explodes into my shoulder, wailing even louder.

"Aw, sweetie," I say and rest my chin on the top of her head.

She cries and cries, almost like she's having seizures, like she's been holding back tears since she was born and now they're loose, running away everywhere like wild, thundering horses. I sit on the sharp gravel, hold her, and wait them out.

"I hurt my ankle," she finally says, calming down. "Bad."

"Should we get you to the hospital?" I ask.

"Yeah," she says. "Oh, fuck. Will you help me get my mother's car back to town, too?"

"Okay," I say. "Keys in it?"

"Yeah."

"I'm going to back it up so you won't have to walk as far." I jog to the car and open the door. The smell of cigarettes and beer nearly knocks me over. I get in anyway, turn the key, and creep up to her. Then I get out, put her arm around my neck, and help her to the backseat. I get back into the driver's seat and drive up the hill to the top of the driveway where Daniel has been waiting with Faith.

"Kelli hurt her ankle," I say to Daniel calmly, "and we need to return her mother's car. Would you be kind enough to follow us to town in your truck?"

Daniel puts Faith in his pickup and follows us.

As I drive to town, Kelli asks, "Did your parents ever hit you?"

I take a big breath. "No."

"What were they like?" she asks.

"My dad died serving his country when I was fourteen. At some point Mom decided we needed to move to a spiritual community where we would help with subsistence farming and tofu production. I hated those bean curds. I ran away and lived with my grandmother for the rest of high school."

"Was your mom mad?" she asks.

"Well, Mom couldn't fault me too much since she was the one who taught me to walk away instead of fight. Like when I was bullied in school, she told me to ignore it and walk away. That didn't work. Yeah, my dad taught me violence isn't the answer, and my mom taught me that running away isn't, either. What did your parents teach you?"

"People who drink whiskey get mean," she says.

"Hm. Yeah, well, if you think about it, people drink whiskey to escape their pain. Maybe the lesson your parents offered you is how much it hurts others when a person tries to escape their own pain," I say, hoping she can hear that I'm trying to encourage her not to run from her child.

"So why aren't we taking your car to your mom's house?" I ask.

"It's a bad scene there," she says.

"Tell me about it," I say.

"Well, tonight I locked Faith and me in the bathroom because I don't have a bedroom. I sleep on the couch. And when my mom and her latest dud boyfriend start fighting, it's important to lock me and Faith somewhere, you know?"

"You're not safe?"

"No." She shakes her head. "Like tonight, she was begging him not to leave. I was watching through the keyhole. She was drunk and standing in front of the door, trying to block him. He jerked the door open, and it smacked her in the side of the face. She fell, and he yelled, 'Get out of the way, bitch!' He pulled the door even wider so that it pushed her into a little ball behind the door. Before he slammed the door, he yelled at me, 'Shut that fucking kid up!' and then my mom started screaming at me, 'This is all because of you, you little whore!' "

I tear up and exhale. "Ouch."

"I didn't care. I don't care what she thinks of me. She's pathetic. After that I watched her lean back against the wall behind the door and then slide right down it and eventually pass out. And then, I don't know, it hit me that I was looking at my future, and if I stayed, Faith could expect a life just like mine. And I looked at myself in the bathroom mirror, at this." She gestures to her fat lip. "And I looked at Faith sitting in her little car seat on the bathroom floor. That's where I put her when I'm afraid to touch her, afraid I'll shake her or hit her. And I thought about how when she woke me up screaming for the fifth time last night, I lost it, and I smacked her just like my mom smacked me."

I take a big breath and try to think of something to say.

Apparently I wasn't quick enough because she looks out the side window and says quietly, "I smacked a little tiny baby, a helpless little baby. And it didn't make her stop screaming, and it didn't make me feel better. It didn't solve anything. The only good that came out of it was that I realized I had to get rid of her."

All that shame. I don't know what to do with all that shame.

Kelli instructs me to park in front of the Elks', which makes me uncomfortable. I get her out of the backseat and help her into the bed of Daniel's pickup, which makes me even more uncomfortable. And from there, we drive her up the hill to the hospital.

DANIEL

I open the door, with Faith in my arms, and notice the sound the record player makes when the needle has run out of songs. I follow the sound, pick up the arm, lay it gently on the rest, and then turn the record player off. I pause to admire the old record player, forty or fifty years old now and still working. None of my CD players have survived even five years. I consider how this music technology might represent our generations. My grandparents were tough. They were built to last. They endured a lot of hard times. Meanwhile, two months of hard times sent Kelli running. But as soon as I think it, I remember the part of Kelli's letter where she said she hit her daughter just like her mother hit her, and I realize it wasn't two months of hard times that had sent Kelli running. It was a lifetime of hard times.

Mara guides Kelli into the downstairs guest bedroom.

"Um . . . I think Faith needs her diaper changed," I say to Mara, although I doubt she has any more of an idea of how to do those things than I do.

"Kelli, you're going to have to coach us," Mara says.

Kelli talks Mara through it while I watch and learn. Then Mara hands Faith to me, and I take her to the kitchen where I try to make heads or tails of the directions on the formula can. She's hungry and mad. I bounce her while I heat the formula and make exaggerated happy faces at her. Then I pour the formula in a bottle, squirt it on my arm like I've seen women do on TV, figure it feels all right to me, and give her the bottle. She devours it. I burp her, and she pukes all over my shoulder.

I carry her upstairs so I can get a new shirt. I set her down on my bed and wonder whether I'm supposed to lay her down on her back or stomach. I lay her down on her back and watch her carefully to make sure she keeps breathing. Then I pick her up and wonder if one day I'll be going to father-daughter events with her when she's older. I imagine attending her graduation and walking her down the aisle at her wedding. I've never considered escorting a daughter down the aisle before. In my imagination it feels good. I feel happy just thinking about it.

I also know it's possible Kelli will take her away long before that. Then I consider it's possible that I might escort Kelli down the aisle. Maybe she'll end up like a daughter to me . . . or at least a little sister.

"I just can't do it," I hear Kelli say to Mara as I walk down the hall.

"It's a really hard job," Mara replies. "I can see you're exhausted."

"I haven't slept in two months."

"Tonight you're going to sleep here. Daniel and I are going to take care of Faith so you can just sleep the whole night and into tomorrow, okay? We'll get some good food into you, keep some ice on this ankle, and get you feeling a little more like yourself. Okay?"

"Okay," Kelli relents.

"You know, I can't make you stay here or stay with your baby if you don't want to," Mara says to her. "If you do want to stay here, we'll help you take care of Faith. When you start to feel like you're going to snap, you can step out and we'll cover for you. If you don't want to live here, our door is always open to you. If you need a break, we're here. Okay? You don't have to make a decision tonight or tomorrow or this week. I think when you've caught up on your sleep, things will look a lot different to you."

Faith starts crying again. "Sometimes I hate her," Kelli confesses to Mara in a whisper. "Sometimes I find myself thinking she ruined my life even though I know I ruined my own life by having her."

Oh, boy.

Mara says, "You know, Kelli, I think every path has a price. Every path. There would have been a price for not having her, too. I mean, there are other women out there thinking they ruined their lives by not having children." Kelli doesn't reply, so Mara tries a different approach. "Sometimes when I'm really tired, I hate teaching. There are days I'm so exhausted that I can't remember what I was thinking when I chose this profession."

"Really?" Kelli asks.

"Really," Mara says. "And then by the end of summer vacation I'm ready to do it all over again. Why don't you sleep for a few days and see how things look?"

"Okay," she says.

Mara meets me in the kitchen and gives me a bewildered look. She takes some leftover lasagna out of the fridge, puts it on a plate, and sticks it in the microwave. "How do you feel about all this?" she whispers to me.

"I kind of like it," I whisper back, smiling at Faith who has just fallen asleep in my arms.

I walk behind Mara as she takes the hot lasagna to Kelli. Kelli has already fallen asleep. "Geez, she looks small. Small and young. She's just a kid herself," I say.

"Yeah. No shit." Mara shakes her head.

MARA

Three nights later Kelli chops cucumbers, tomatoes, cilantro, and green onion for the tabouli salad while Daniel sets the table and I fry up falafel balls. Faith fusses, so Daniel picks her up and gives her a bottle. Bluegrass music fills the house, making silence between us warm and comfortable. We're taking it day by day, but I suspect Kelli is staying.

Zeus barks, Faith cries, and I notice headlights coming up the driveway. "Can you watch this?" I ask Kelli. She hops over on one foot and takes the spatula from me.

I wipe my hands on my apron and walk out the back door. The beams of light are coming from a VW Bus. I smile. Adam.

He parks, gets out, and walks over to me. His smile and his aura light up the whole yard.

"Welcome!" I call out to him.

"It's so nice to see you again," he says.

I put my arms around his neck and kiss him.

In the middle of the night Faith wakes me up. I walk outside with the child in my arms. Climbing roses have sprung up all around the entrance of our home. I take it as a good sign.

I hear a waltz about angels out of nowhere, like I do in my dancing dreams. Across the yard Edith and Earl smile at me and waltz. I step out into the yard, baby in my arms, and join them.

A PENGUIN READERS GUIDE TO

CHURCH OF THE DOG

Kaya McLaren

An Introduction to
Church of the Dog

After coming to the startling conclusion that her fiancé was not really the man she wanted him to be (*that man* would pay the $10 to get her to the hospital when she is ill), Mara O'Shaunnessey abandons everything—her feisty grandmother, her job, her home, and her garden (carefully transplanted to her grandmother's yard)—to take a position as an art teacher in a small farming community in rural Oregon. Excited to start all over again, Mara immediately makes herself at home; despite having nowhere to live, she has already acquired a companion, Harvey, a pig she rescues from certain doom at the local livestock fair.

With Harvey and the rest of her worldly possessions in tow, Mara is drawn to a ranch on the edge of town, the home of Earl and Edith McRae. Earl and Edith are busy people. Running their ranch, after all, takes a lot of energy—spiritual, physical, and emotional. And at first it seems that they don't have time for someone like Mara, though Earl begrudgingly rents her the old cabin behind the McRaes' own house.

But keeping busy is the only way the McRaes can keep their minds off the tragedies that have visited them. The indescribable heartbreak of losing a child. How much they miss their only grandson, Daniel. Keeping busy, though, also prevents indulging in frivolities—like dancing, laughing, and enjoying their time together.

As Mara sets about fixing up her little cabin, Earl and Edith become more and more enchanted by their new tenant. The moment she finishes up the mural of a dog she's painted on the side of her house, the very dog depicted shows up during a thunderstorm. Edith finds herself compelled to do things she never expected to be doing at this stage of her life. Of course, making snow angels while naked and taking kamikaze horseback missions into town in the middle of the night isn't something she thought she'd do at *any* stage of her life. Earl and Edith find themselves dancing each night in their parlor, roses woven into Edith's hair, just like when they met. But what is Mara really? A witch, a shaman, a healer, a guardian angel? No matter, Earl and Edith are having too much fun to wonder for long.

The McRaes' beloved grandson, Daniel, has been leading a life of his own since the day he fled to Alaska. Scarred by the death of his parents, Daniel has always been much better at running away than facing the disappointment on his grandparents' faces. Despite all these years of near silence, his grandparents write regularly to ask him to come home. And until now he has always refused, content to forget what he was once supposed to be and concentrate on what he has become—a fisherman. But this letter feels different. This time his grandfather even says "please." There are more than just fences that need mending.

What Daniel finds on the ranch astonishes him. Edith and Earl laughing more, flirting more, loving more. In fact, there are so many changes, all connected to Mara, that the ranch does not seem like the oppressive place he ran away from. Now it feels like a place of happiness, safety, and stability.

But this happiness, as Daniel is terribly aware, is fragile: Earl is gravely ill.

As Mara and Daniel become partners in running the ranch, she must help him finally make peace with his past and future. Mara knows no being passes through this life without making a difference for good or for ill. But as Daniel lashes out as the awful memories of the past begin to visit the present and Mara feels the powers she has relied upon for so long begin to fail her, she wonders if she has ever really been able to do any good at all. How can Mara hope to change this grown man whose emotions are so tangled? The clarity both Daniel and Mara seek arrives unexpectedly with a strange cry that splits the night. And suddenly the two are tied together as family, a clear future of both sorrow and joy spreading out before them.

About Kaya McLaren

Kaya McLaren teaches art and lives on the east slope of Snoqualmie Pass in Washington state with her dog, Big Cedar. Her second novel, *On the Divinity of Second Chances*, will be published by Penguin in winter 2009.

A Conversation with
Kaya McLaren

Your descriptions of day-to-day life on a ranch are incredibly evocative. Do you have experience working on ranches? Did you grow up in that environment?

I didn't grow up on a ranch. I wanted to. For a while when I was a kid, I did have a pony, and then later a horse. I rode my bike out to take care of them every day. There's nothing like a good horse—nothing. After I no longer had a horse, I simply rode any horse anyone would let me ride. I still do. I was a horse instructor at a summer camp for a short time and I worked as a guide on a dude ranch, too. I had a horse a few years ago. She nearly killed me, though, so I sold her to a breeding farm. Now she just eats grass and gets lucky.

Mary Roberts is a rancher in Montana I interviewed. She's the reason behind the great details. My second cousin Robin not only put me in touch with Mary, but also answered some of my questions. Robin and her husband are bucking bull breeders and stock contractors. Glimpses into their world are always a treat for me.

What elements of the book, particularly with regard to Mara's intuitive powers, are drawn from your own experience? Are any of the characters based on people in your life?

This is an uncomfortable question for me. I started writing *Church of the Dog* on a snow day when my TV was broken. It was too cold to go to the back part of the house where I painted and made stained glass. I thought it might be fun to write a book and think of it like a painting. I didn't keep any of my paintings then. I just liked the experience of painting. Naturally, I figured I wouldn't keep the book.

So, in the beginning, it was just sort of a vacation into a warmer imaginary place that was based on the community where I was living and who I was at the time. What would it be like if I lived behind someone's house and wasn't alone? What would it be like if I had supernatural powers? What would it have been like if I could have adopted my student's pig? And wouldn't it be great if I was given a horse and had a place to keep it? The book was largely my dream at that point in my life, not so much my reality. Sure, the way I viewed the world at that time is very much woven into the book. Since I didn't intend to publish it, it ended up being a much more personal book than I would have written if I knew I was writing for an audience.

As far as intuitive powers, I get asked that question a lot. I never know how to answer it. I've never shrunk a tumor, if that's what you're wondering.

How do you go about "weeding"? What advice would you give to others about how to find activities and philosophies to cultivate a rich life while weeding out the negatives?

I'm no master of this. My closet is evidence of that. I do notice that I tend to handle negativity by moving, like I might get on my bike and ride and ride and ride, or I might ski really fast. I might sing loud or dance around my house. When my physical body isn't clear, for me, nothing is clear. Feng shui is a fun exercise in intention. I do like the idea of allowing our physical reality reflect our commitment to different ideas, intentions, and dreams. I also like to write my prayers all over my shower walls in soap crayon. That's one way I ask for help "weeding," reflect on gratitude, and commit to what kind of force I want to be in the world. I notice other people clean their houses to "weed." I wish I had a little more of that in me.

Why did you choose to structure the book with the four different narrators? Do you think it made the book easier or more difficult to write? How do you go about creating these four individual personalities and their voices?

I think I was contemplating how it is that we all have such different realities in this world, and yet, all things considered, we coexist pretty peacefully. It's easy to think that the rest of your family or the rest of your community shares your perceptions. I'm here to tell you that they don't. Was it hard to write? No. In fact, I really enjoyed it. It allowed me to weave together the wide spectrum of perceptions that are all inside me. I mean, if you ask my best friend who I am most like, she might tell you I'm actually more like Earl than Mara. I can be pretty cranky.

Please describe how you go about writing. Is there a particular place where you feel most in tune with your characters? Are there certain times of the day when it comes easiest for you?

I wrote this book in the bathtub. Ha, ha, ha! You just read a book I wrote naked! I called my bath tub "my office." I wrote longhand in a three-ring binder. Computers are too dangerous in the bathtub.

Nowadays, I proofread in the bathtub, but I write up in my loft. I love to write late at night. I always listen to music when I write. Sometimes I'll listen to the same song over and over for a while if it helps keep me in the right space. While I wrote *Church of the Dog*, I must have listened to Bruce Springsteen's "The Ghost of Tom Joad" a thousand times. It's quiet, simple, acoustic, and a little melancholy. I'm not good at writing in chronological order. I skip all around and write whatever I feel like. Then I weave it together. In a way, it creates an interesting framework to fill in as I go. I'm trying to make myself be a little more linear these days. I think it will improve flow and continuity if I could do that. You hear about writers who sit down and write in a really disciplined way. That sounds like so much non-fun, I can't begin to tell you. If the book is a chore to write, it might be a chore to read, too. Ew. I write because I love writing. Sometimes I write when I'm trying to make or find peace in a certain situation. Usually, I write because it's fun. I hope my books are fun to read because they were written with that spirit and spontaneity.

Since you are an art teacher and a dog owner, it seems natural to surmise that the character of Mara O'Shaunnessey is based in part on yourself. Did you intend to write a character that contained aspects of your personality? How important is art in your own life? Does your own home resemble the Church of the Dog?

I'd love it if my house did look like the Church of the Dog! I live in a little log house now. I love it. Visual art has been getting neglected in my life lately because I'm going through a really powerful writing time. I only had one painting night in the last two years. It was fabulous, though. Creating visual art is profoundly calming to me. It clears my mind. It helps me lose judgment about troubles, and see my life more like a canvas, a work-in-progress, an imperfect, but beautiful creation.

The other part of the question I feel like I already answered. It needs to be said that I wrote this book ten years ago. I was twenty-eight. I hope I'm not the same person I was when I was twenty-eight. I hope I've evolved into a gentler and more graceful person. I hope I'm more compassionate and less judgmental than I was ten years ago. I hope my capacity for love is greater. I hope every year I grow in that way. That's the uncomfortable part about creating something and having it go to press; it freezes a moment in time and may or may not reflect the truth as I understand it in the future.

It's possible for books to become like shoes we've outgrown.

Mara has deep interest in her students and is dismayed when they have troubles. Do you think schools in this country are failing to nurture students? What improvements do you think should be made?

Do I think the schools are failing to nurture students? My first thought was, what do we mean when we say the schools? The teachers I know are very, very committed and caring people who would walk through fire for any one of their students. The administrators I've known have all wanted the students in their school to have unlimited possibilities available to them as they progress through life.

Education in the United States is tricky. I think there are few, if any, other places in the world where an educational system accommodates such a wide spectrum of cultures, values, and ability levels. Most educational systems in the world don't strive to educate *everybody*. Standardized testing has become paramount in our systems, and yes, that does break my heart sometimes. There are so many strengths a person can embody which are not strengths that can be measured and represented with a numerical value. How sad to have an eight-year-old look at a number and think, "I'm below average," and potentially carry that limiting thought pattern with him the rest of his life. I do not feel good about participating in that aspect of the educational system.

The bigger question to me is, "Is our culture failing to nurture children?" I would like to see an end to the glamorization of violence in our culture reflected in the media. I would like to see a slower pace for our children, where they have time to make up their own games, use their imagination, and explore nature instead of going from one structured activity to another. I would like to see a culture for children that downplayed competition and emphasized cooperation. Maybe by overemphasizing competition, we actually teach children to be cruel to others and themselves. I don't know. I would like a culture for children where it is believed that any child who is doing their best is succeeding. I would like to see a culture for children that challenged them to create their own entertainment rather than rely on the latest gadget for it. How do we tell our children that they have enough and they are enough and that they're beautiful, when thousands of commercials a week, their peers, our standardized tests, and sometimes coaches tell them the opposite? That's what I love about summer camp. At summer camp, it's enough just to be a nice kid.

Please tell us more about your relationships with your four-legged companions. Have your pets found you, or did you actively seek them out?

I saw an ad for Tasha Good Dog, my first dog, in the newspaper when I was working archaeology. There was a creepy guy on my crew that made me wonder if I should have a gun. I thought a dog would be more fun than a gun, so I looked for the biggest, scariest, free, full-grown one I could find. As it turned out, she got carsick, so taking her to work every day on these Forest Service roads wasn't going to work for any of us. After a day or two of that, I packed her up and pursued teaching. In that way, she did protect me from the creepy guy, just not in the way I expected. Ha! Life is so funny like that.

I picked up my current dog, Big Cedar, at a shelter. There was a night where I couldn't stop thinking that I had to go there. I went the next day. I was looking for something with a little sled dog in it since I'm such a snow person, and he wasn't that. He's a German Shepherd-yellow Lab mix. I was also looking for a female, and he wasn't that either. But while the other dogs in the shelter went nuts, jumping up and down and barking at me, he just sat there and looked at me. He said to me earnestly in plain telepathic English, "I'm the BEST one."

Well, what are you going to do when a dog tells you he's the best one? You take him home.

What are you working on now?

Right now I'm finishing my third book, *How I Came to Sparkle Again,* and sometimes I pick up the manuscript of my fourth novel. *Sparkle* takes place in a ski town, in ski culture. It explores a couple themes: how does the nature of men and women differ in the context of love and how do we have relationships with loved ones when their religious convictions override their respect for us?

In my fourth book, I entertain the idea that if Jesus were to reincarnate, the people who profess to love him the most might be the least likely to recognize him. Is anyone else so very tired of hateful bigots pretending to be do-gooders? I'm so tired of everyone thinking God likes them best and that everyone else is going to hell. That's ridiculous.

Questions for Discussion

1. If you could travel in your sleep, where would you go? What companions would you like to accompany you?

2. Daniel wonders if "the only way to freedom is through devastation." He cites the Revolutionary War as a path for freedom for America, the Civil War as a path to freedom for slaves, a dam crumbling to release a river. What are some other instances where renewal comes from destruction? Are there are other ways to reach freedom and renewal? What are they?

3. Discuss the significance of Mara's dual visions of her students' futures (p. 174–175).

4. Mara isn't sure she has had an impact on her students. What are your vivid memories of teachers that influenced your own life? Which ones made a positive difference in your life? Negative? How?

5. Daniel is angry that the funerals of his mother and father, and later, his grandfather, seem insulting to the very people they are meant to honor. Who are funerals really for, the living or the dead? Should clergy respect the varied religious traditions that might be represented or tailor services to fit only the religion of the deceased?

6. Edith can't seem to give Earl's clothes and effects away and her son's room is still as he left it. She reflects that her mother

got rid of all Edith's father's personal items almost immediately after his death. Which way of coping with a death do you think is healthier? Why? Are there items that remind you of people or events, things you have thought about letting go of but have not?

7. Mara questions Daniel about his negatives—photographic negatives, that is. What are some projects you have not seen through? Why did you abandon them? Do you think you will ever see them through to completion?

8. Kelli attempts to abandon her newborn with Mara and Daniel. How would you react if someone tried to leave a baby with you? Would you react in the same way that Mara and Daniel do? Could you open your home to someone who in Kelli's situation, despite the possibility of it affecting your own life in a significant way?

9. In her dreams, Mara has traveled near the edge of Heaven several times. Is this aspect of Mara's personality believable? Is Mara truly in Heaven, or is it just a construct of her own imagination? What do you picture when you think of Heaven?

10. Mara collects quite a few pets through the course of the novel, beginning with Harvey, her pig. What personality traits do you look for in a dog or other sort of pet? In a friend? In what ways do they overlap? Would you consider any of your pets a guardian angel?

11. The author chose to use four different narrators in *Church of the Dog*, Mara, Earl, Edith, and Daniel. Did you find that you missed one of the characters after they stopped telling the story from their point of view? What character did you become most attached to during the course of the novel?

For more information about or to order other Penguin Readers Guides, please e-mail the Penguin Marketing Department at reading@us.penguingroup.com or write to us at:

Penguin Books Marketing Dept.
Readers Guides
375 Hudson Street
New York, NY 10014-3657

Please allow 4–6 weeks for delivery.
To access Penguin Readers Guides online, visit the Penguin Group (USA) Inc. Web site at www.penguin.com and www.vpbookclub.com

COMING IN WINTER 2009
FROM PENGUIN BOOKS

On the Divinity of Second Chances

KAYA McLAREN

Kaya McLaren celebrates moments of pure beauty and wonder in her second novel. Overflowing with unforgettable characters, it revels in the miracle of second chances as it follows one family and their search for true contentment. As the only family member with any perspective, Jade knows that her brother Forrest has gone into hiding to atone for an accident he caused many years before. She also knows that her straight-laced sister Olive has a secret that could end her parents' already unstable marriage. *On the Divinity of Second Chances* is a lively, magical tale of love and family that reminds us that everyone has a second chance, and that sometimes that second chance is even better than the first.

**Penguin
Books**